COVER THIS COUNTRY LIKE SNOW

COVER THIS COUNTRY LIKE SNOW

and
Other Stories

KRISTINE ZEIGLER

Pupfish Press, California

Pupfish Press
1547 Palos Verdes Mall, #165
Walnut Creek, CA 94597
Copyright © Kristine Zeigler, 2018
All rights reserved

Love Me Tender

Publisher's Note

978-1-7329044-0-8 (pbk.)

Library of Congress Control Number: 2018961441

Book Design by Ian Koviak & Alan Dino Hebel of *the*BookDesigners
Author Portrait by Kira Stackhouse

To Joe

My Love

The Author

KRISTINE ZEIGLER is a third-generation California writer who grew up in the rural communities of Bishop and Mammoth Lakes in the Eastern Sierra Nevada Mountains. Zeigler's previous publication credits include *Forge Journal, The Bark, The Peregrine, Charles River Review, Menda City Review, Ignatian Literary Magazine, Barely South Review,* and *The Saint Ann's Review.* Zeigler previously reported on energy and toxic waste laws and regulations in Washington, D.C. For the past twenty years, Zeigler has been an environmental non-profit leader focused on preserving nature with, and for, people. Zeigler was awarded a writer residency at the H.J. Andrews Experimental Forest as part of an Oregon State University and U.S. Forest Service program to promote understanding of humanity's role in nature. She serves as a member of the board of directors of the Mono Lake Committee and blogs about natural and cultural history. A graduate of Lafayette College, Zeigler lives in the San Francisco Bay Area with her husband Joe and rescue dog Connor. She holds a private pilot's license and flies a Cessna 182.

Contents

Nomenclatura

In life, it's not heroism that matters as much as consistency and good sense. At least in life as it's lived, not life as it is chronicled much later when heroism seems to trump pragmatism. Around an evening's fire in the High Sierra wilderness before Christmas in 1845 sat two kinds of men—storied, charismatic men like Captain John Charles Frémont and men about whom we don't know a thing, like Milton Williams.

Milton Williams never commanded the stage, though he played his part. Along the way he left his trace—a couple of painted crosses on granite boulders telling those who came after, *I was here.* But now those markings, hidden by lichen or blasted by dynamite, are as forgotten as Milton, just rubble along a highway interstate. Yet Milton was the sort people counted on and knew better than the glory seekers whose names appear on bronze disks at mountain summits or on maps as names of rivers and long valleys. Nothing is named for Milton in the great valley. Not even a modest peak or meadow. A real shame too, since he did more on that topographical expedition of the West than did the valley's namesake, Richard Owens.

Richard Owens towered over a pack mule. He had broad shoulders and an angle to him that said he was tough, smart, and didn't fare too shabbily with women. He had a way of looking at a situation and seeing the way through with a steady, studied glance. He always had another man's back—this time John Charles Frémont and Kit Carson, the intrepid mountain man and guide.

But back to Milton. He was stationed at the river, keeping an eye on the Indians who occasionally moved from hut to hut carrying long, oval baskets on their backs. Milton thought he heard an Indian baby cry out but then thought it might be a coyote pup. The high-pitched wail reminded him of the expedition's families who they would soon leave behind with Joseph Reddeford Walker. Yes, that Walker. Walker River, Walker Pass, Walker Lake. Walker was arguing with Frémont.

"But we know a good route to get us to the southern end of the Sierra and can do it in eleven or twelve days, avoiding the snow and cold completely," Walker said to Frémont. Walker's eyebrows rose and seemed to indicate that anyone who did not follow him would be foolish and impractical. But Frémont wanted to split up and take his smaller, more nimble party over the pass he had crossed the winter before. The heart of the snowy range beckoned, and Frémont would listen.

"The weather's looking just fine, Walker," Frémont said.

"I don't know how you can see into the future, sir, but it would be a terrible risk. You know that. Come with us. With me, you won't be eating any dogs or mules. My route through the long valley, well below the snow, is sensible and far more pleasurable," Walker said.

"We'll see you at Tulare Lake, Walker. It will be Christmas soon, so let's share one more meal together. We'll open some of the whiskey and ask Milton to play his fiddle."

Milton kept the party awake until early morning, singing Irish and English tunes that everyone knew.

Long after the festivities ended, a shout from the edge of the dying firelight interrupted the party's quiet preparations for the night.

"Someone's hurt," Owens said. The men grabbed their guns and ran to the river's edge. Owens could hear the river before he could see it. In the moon's eggshell brightness, trees and nearby peaks formed a pretty silhouette. He made out a figure on the ground, a man clutching his thigh. As he approached, he saw an arrow lodged in the man's ample left leg.

"I don't know what happened, Dick," Milton said, his breath incomplete and his groans requiring more air than he could obtain. "There's a bear nearby. I could hear it run."

"It's probably run away. In consequence of you being shot, we are to move you. Carson, lift his feet and I'll get his arms," Owens ordered.

"Don't touch me! Must be the sharpest obsidian point ever made."

"Shush, you! Don't draw more attention. Those Indians are good shots," Owens said. Kit Carson looked at the shaft. "Must have been carved for bear hunting," he said. "Owens," he said, cupping his palm about his ear, "that bear's not far away. Hurry." Carson and Owens carried Milton back to the firelight. As they rolled Milton on to his right side to keep the arrow from touching the ground, the heft of a hulking animal snared itself on branches and bushes across the river. Owens did not have time to fetch his rifle. He could not see the marauding shadow but knew its breath and chuff. He slid his revolver from its leather holster and cocked the hammer back. The animal, he could now see, was a grizzly, barreling ever closer.

"You just go ahead and try to kill me," Owens said, raising his right arm and aiming at the behemoth. The bear stopped to get a better view of things, standing on its hind legs at the edge of the water. It was nearly as tall as a covered wagon, the tallest bear Owens had ever seen. It had plentiful, shaggy fur and claws as long as Spanish daggers. Owens eyed the bear's chest and fired twice. The bear fell forward. Owens stood still, confident that the bear would soon desist. But the bear roared again, bared its teeth, and pushed its wide paws into the rocky banks, charging toward the camp. Owens aimed again and pulled the trigger but the gun did not fire. He felt for more bullets in his leather pouch, but his clumsy fingers prevented him from finding them. The bear would soon have his heart. As he turned and ran to the camp, he realized he was leading the bear to the other men as well, but he was unable to do otherwise. He cried out to Carson as he tripped on a saddle that he could not see. Before the bear could pounce on him, it reared up and turned, away from Owens and toward the river, heading down to a sandy shore, howling piteously. Owens got up from the ground. Kit Carson reached down to pull him up.

"Close call there, Dick," Carson said.

"Thanks for shooting him," Owens said.

"Nah, wasn't me, Dick. It was Milton. He has eagle eyesight. Saw the bastard was after you and pulled the revolver out of his pants. Hell of a shot."

"He got up with that arrow in his leg?"

"Well, I suppose he did," Carson said.

"Admirable," Owens said. "Suppose I am in his debt now."

"Suppose you are," Carson said. He raised a lantern toward the river. The bear continued to snort and groan for several minutes. At last it took one last gasp, lifted its unwieldy head, and sighed long like a melancholy flute. Eventually, its whole body sank beneath the surface of the water.

The next morning, Captain Frémont rose early with first light and found the bear two miles downriver, stuck in an eddy between several glassy granite slabs, some uneven river bottom, and the shore. Flies buzzed around its nose and eyes. It was monumental and proud, grander than any bear he had seen. It surely could have killed every man, woman, and child in the camp. *I'll need ten men and a horse with a wagon to move this bear to the mess wagon*, Captain Frémont thought to himself. *The cook will prepare it for supper*. The captain stared at the lifeless body in the shallow water. He turned and walked slowly back to the camp, took a handkerchief from his pocket, and wiped his brow. Even in death's repose the bear seemed to threaten them all. He wondered if the animal was a sign of bad luck. Though the sun was higher now, it had grown colder and began to snow.

When Frémont returned to fetch the bear with his men, Indians had gathered on the opposite shore. Frémont counted. Eleven men and four squaws. None appeared to have a weapon. Snow and wind assailed them and yet the Indians remained, unmoving. Frémont called to them. "No trouble today, Chief," he yelled over the din of the rapids that boomed between them.

The Indians did not hear. What they saw were the men who had stolen their bear and killed it with the thunder hand smoke. But they also had seen their arrow pierce the watchman, and this made them nervous. The white men would certainly take the bear now, though it was not rightfully theirs. So they stood as witnesses while the bear was removed from the river and carted off by the heaving and huffing white men. The Chief gestured for Walker to cross the river, as he knew a few of their words.

The Chief explained that the bear was theirs and that the arrow in the white man was a mistake. They would settle for less than the whole bear, the Chief said.

"I will take the shoulder of the giant beast, it will be enough to feed my people," the Chief said. Walker crossed the river back to the men, who had stilled themselves to catch their breath.

"They want some of the bear to eat," Walker said.

"They'll have none," said Frémont. "They tried to kill Milton, and we won't have them eating the spoils of this kill," he said.

"But sir, if we do not comply, they may take revenge," Walker said.

"Against all of us? There's hardly a dozen men, and all they have are arrows," Frémont said.

"Sir, I hate to disagree, but in this case I feel that the safety of our numbers is in danger if we do not cede at least the flanks and shoulder of this beast to them."

"Walker, just help us get this ugly creature back to camp," Frémont said.

By the time the men returned, they were walking in four inches of snow and the sky was full of the storm, the sun blocked out by bland, gray, flat clouds.

The cook carved up the bear and divided the meat equally. Brief but poignant speeches of parting, followed by exchanges of luck and Godspeed, made them feel a sense of ceremony and hopefulness mixed with the impending emptiness that comes with separation. Walker glanced back and forth between Frémont and his departing men and the anvil clouds in the slate-colored sky. It seemed inevitable that storms would swallow beasts and men whole. With the Frémont expedition out of sight, Walker removed the meat from the back of the wagon, wrapped a blanket around it, and slung it over his horse, tying it up around the horn. He rode back to the Indians and when he arrived on the opposite shore, he called to the Chief, who stepped out of his dwelling. Walker hurled the meat to the ground, turned his horse and galloped back to camp.

The next day Walker led his party along the river banks until they reached the headwaters of a longer, more majestic desert river flowing through one of the most dramatic landscapes yet to be discovered.

"Perhaps," he said out loud to no one in particular, "this river will one day enchant all men."

One month later the two parties reunited. Inside a tent pitched at the southern end of the San Joaquin Valley, Captain Frémont raised his glass to Richard Owens. "To a brave, courageous, and fine shot." Carson and Owens looked at one another. They decided against correcting their leader just then. Milton, after all, had perished some weeks earlier. An infection, it was said.

"To a man who saved men, women, and children from the deadly grizzly bear of the Sierra," Frémont continued. "A man of integrity and sound judgment in the face of danger. In his honor, I have named the long desert valley traveled by Walker and his brave families. The river and its terminal lake shall also bear his name. I propose this toast to Richard Owens, a man I hope to have by my side forevermore. May the Owens Valley, Owens River, and Owens Lake henceforth proudly bear the name of one of the nation's most daring and brilliant men."

The officers raised their glasses and talked about the promise of a week's pause.

Joseph Reddeford Walker shook his head and exited the tent to gaze at the full moon. In the distance, he could see the western face of the Sierra foothills, small mounds in comparison to the jagged peaks that lay on the other side. He inhaled the soft air and downed his whiskey. Just then he caught sight of an unmistakable shape. A grizzly. It stood on all four legs, watching Walker. Walker raised his glass to the bear. He could see two small cubs at her feet. She lifted her glistening nose and seemed to spend a moment ascertaining the number of men inside the tent. Deciding against any further action, she encouraged her offspring in the opposite direction, away from the camp and toward the murky grasslands.

Walker returned to the reunion, not mentioning the sighting to anyone. They had plenty of meat from the antelope and black bear killed that past week during their sojourn down the valley on the eastern side of the Sierra. Which apparently had a new name. The wrong one, but a name nonetheless.

"Owens Valley. Not bad," Walker said, patting Richard Owens on the back. Owens laughed.

"Doubt it will stick, such an empty land," Owens said. Owens then yelled out to Kit Carson, who passed by carrying a bottle of whiskey under his arm.

"Come Mr. Carson. Join us for a toast," Owens said.

"Be obliged," Carson said, pouring a dram for Walker, then Owens, then for himself.

"To Milton," Owens said.

"To Milton," Carson and Walker said in unison.

Cover This Country Like Snow

The boy walked in the waning light, unaware that the cold had spread across his hairless skin and that the mild, cloying warmth that day was no indication the season was at an end. He did not notice that the heavy, dull air of winter was still in the sky, was cradled by the mountains. He did not foretell the snow that would come and break upon the ground for forty-two more days and nights. Determined to find his friend, the boy swung himself over a low fence and a pile of fresh-cut pine lumber. The stream of the sun began to disappear behind the hulking ridge of the eastern side of the Sierra Nevada range as he crouched inside a new corral in what is now known as Round Valley. For months he had taken this same path to get to Mister Billy, a young steer belonging to Lefty McAuliffe. Lefty didn't mind that the boy, who he called George, was so often about the place. A slight Paiute of uncertain age, his skin too soft to yet be a man, with eyes that seemed to view a world beyond this one and hands expressing themselves in constant movement like a ribbon of water, this George was different, a bit aloof but altogether harmless. Every now and then Lefty would yell at George to "Git," as he had so much to do and George's presence slowed him down. Lefty did not always tolerate the lingering stare, at once as empty as it was full, of this boy, or almost man, this dumb Indian.

George wondered what had changed. Quail, rabbits, and giant sagebrush here yesterday. Today, dusty saddles slung over new posts and metallic feed troughs brimming with hay. He stood and found his Mister Billy, a red-brown Hereford with a white face, a silken hide, and eyes bordered by patches of pale pink skin and gray eyelashes. Mister Billy swished his long tail in greeting.

"Who took the sage? Where did the rabbit run to?" George asked.

"Don't rightly know," said the steer. Mister Billy lowered his neck in vain toward what should have been spring grasses pushing through the soil. It was past the time when George's father would dig out his ditches to water the wild hyacinths and yellow nut grass.

George placed his palm alongside the sturdy animal's neck and ran it over the brown skin toward the leg. George liked this new cow breed so recently brought to his valley home. It was gentler than mule deer, did not mind being petted, and liked to have a conversation every evening. He then scratched Mister Billy where the steer's hair curled tightly behind the ears.

Mister Billy pulled hay into his mouth and ground it against his back teeth, the mixing of saliva turning the alfalfa into a satisfying delicacy. His chewing slowed, his eyelids closed, and he began to dream, a talent given to all hoofed animals but perfected by bovines. Mister Billy saw a two-legged creature with a desert-colored fur coat and a full tail.

Shall I warn the others? Mister Billy wondered.

"Hello, Mister Billy. Lovely evening tonight."

"Coyote?"

"Yes, it's a strange sight, isn't it, me on two legs? I have come to give you news, Mister Billy, and it isn't the kind of news one delivers on four legs, if you know what I mean."

"So you've come to bring the warning call?"

"Yes, Mister Billy. I am the emissary of Eagle, and he has foreseen a battle that will begin tonight."

"Will this battle put my herd in harm's way?"

"Mister Billy, you will be the cause of the battle."

"But I hold no ill feelings toward any men!"

"That is of no consequence. Mister Billy, your George will be by your side when it happens, and he will be the one harmed."

"Is there anything I can do to change this?"

"You can try, but it has been foretold and Eagle is never wrong."

"You've pulled tricks like this before, Coyote."

"But I come on two legs. I cannot lie, Mister Billy."

"You speak truth. I can see it in your eyes and your taut whiskers. Thank you, Coyote. I must gather the others and leave the corral. We'll hide until after nightfall. Perhaps George will forget me."

"Mister Billy, I doubt it will work."

Before the steer could argue otherwise, Coyote fell to all four legs and was soon gone.

When Mister Billy awoke, he felt the cud in his mouth and George's warm, steady hand on his back. He blinked and then remembered Coyote's warning. Mister Billy shook George's hand free.

"Cows, calves, and steers, we must head to the canyon! Now!" He scraped his hoof against the chalky dirt and issued a long lowing command that awakened all of the cattle from their twilight dreams and stirred in each of them a desire to obey.

George leaped out of the herd's way. The frenetic cattle stampeded behind Mister Billy, stirring up dust and rocks as they disappeared behind a stand of trees at the edge of George's vision. George, paralyzed by fear that he had done something terribly wrong, began to worry that the cows were in danger. He waited until the moon rose and then set out to find Mister Billy. George, fast as a deer, filled his lungs with long draws of the mountain's air. His feet gripped the face of the granite valley as easily as those of a bighorn sheep, ascending the canyon's boulders and dodging the icy patches alongside the stream. He ran and he ran, bent on finding his friend and not noticing his hunger or thirst or taxed muscles. He did not stop until he saw the dim hulking shadows of the cattle.

"Oh, Mister Billy, there you are!" George threw his arms around the steer's neck. "I thought you were angry at me."

"I'm not upset at all. We are merely taking precautions. I spoke to Coyote. You must leave as you are in danger, my George. Go and continue, as far as you can. Your legs are still strong."

"But why?"

"The battle is coming. I've heard of others. Bloody gunfights. Many vanquished. So many brown men dead. So many white men dead. I don't know, George. Your people, what match are they for greater numbers and their guns?"

George placed his right hand on Mister Billy's neck as they ambled up the canyon beneath the spindly branches of aspen trees stretching for remnant light. "George, the white men are like stars above our heads. They are the sands in the Owens River. You can take away sand, but more will come. There are many, many wrongs. But can you climb Mount Tom and extinguish the light from the stars?" George admitted he could not.

"George, how will you gather enough guns, powder, lead, dried meat for your warriors, and fresh grass to feed your horses? Your enemies have all of these and far more than they can ever use."

"I don't have enemies!" George shouted. His eyes were glistening, reflecting the pulse of the stars.

"The army of white men," Mister Billy whispered, "will cover this country like snow."

As the two silenced their voices and listened to the

water washing over flattened stones, a cowboy named Lawrence Jones spotted a stolen Hereford with an Indian man, aimed his rifle at the tall shadow standing next to the McAuliffe-branded steer, and fired. The bullet traveled through George's heart, puncturing it so efficiently that he scarcely felt it as he fell. He wondered why he did not see Mister Billy. Then he was summoned to the Great Camp in the sky, where he would wait for his father, content in the warm protection of his mother, his grandfather, and all of his mothers and fathers before that.

Mister Billy, startled by the shot, ran toward the creek, stumbled into the glacial waters, and landed awkwardly in a small eddy. He raised his head to gain his bearings and saw Lawrence Jones kneeling by George, shaking the dead boy's shoulder. Jones' and Mister Billy's eyes met, and Jones released George and barked at Mister Billy, "Ignorant steer, get the hell up. We got to get back to Lefty's!"

Mister Billy was able to right himself and wade out of the creek and back up to the trail. He paused over George's body and sniffed the death that had overtaken his lean rabbit-running muscles. Mister Billy shook his head, walked behind the cowboy, and sighed. Coyote was right. The battle was beginning. "I've failed you," Mister Billy said as the cowboy hauled George up on his mount, where the blood of the boy flowed into the sweat of the horse.

Lawrence Jones knew his boss, Lefty McAuliffe, would be pleased. The Indians had gone far enough. They had killed at least three head of cattle this winter and this would have been the fourth. *The boy would have killed Lefty's cow and fed on it for weeks,* he thought. *Well, no sir, not on my watch.* "I had begun to suspicion," he whispered, "so I took care of it."

The rest of the confused cattle huddled near the bottom of the creek. Lawrence set to the task of driving them back into the valley.

It was well past supper when Lawrence Jones stood near Lefty's kitchen window, hoping the missus would invite him to sit down for mutton broth and a plate of fish. Lefty appeared inside, his cheeks glowing from the heated water his wife had brought for his toilet. In the kitchen lantern's glow, Lawrence saw the L-shaped scar beneath Lefty's ear, the skin pink like the pads of a kitten's paw. An Indian arrow, it was widely known, had narrowly missed the spot that brings blood to the head but had inscribed its traces on the side of Lefty's neck nonetheless. Lefty strode through the kitchen to the hall that led to the back door, brushing his wife aside to give a vigorous shake to his hired man's hand. Lawrence Jones requested a moment alone just to talk a little business, a proposition that Lefty enjoyed hearing very much for he was on the lookout for men who thought about the ranching enterprise as much as he did.

"Cold night, isn't it, Lawrence? I hope summer comes here soon. Been a long and cruel winter for all of us. Twenty days of snow since May. Here it is halfway into June already. Nothing like this in New York, I can tell you that. This is frozen heartbreak," Lefty said.

Lawrence nodded and shifted his gaze outside to a stand of cottonwoods planted at the edge of the road. "Sir, I got something to show you."

Lefty and Lawrence walked to the figure propped up against the trunk of the largest tree in the yard. Lefty squatted to get a better look.

"Good God, what have we got here?" Lefty pulled George's matted hair away. "Lawrence, you gone and killed yourself a crazy Indian child!"

"Thought you'd be proud," Lawrence said.

"This boy never gives us any problems! He don't even talk. He just walks around the ranch and mumbles to the cows and horses. I even put him to work a few times. You gone and killed a harmless pest is what you done." The obsidian sky concealed the color vanishing from Lawrence's face.

"But sir," Lawrence stammered, "he was taking the cows up the ravine. He was stealing your cows. Taking advantage. I've been on the job one month only, but I seen how they been taking the cows. They're living off the fat provided by us and it ain't fair, sir."

"George couldn't steal a cow. He wouldn't have known what to do with it. He couldn't barely get by in this world. He had a touch of the melancholy like," Lefty said. "Didn't even speak in his own tongue," he added with a sigh.

"Ah, hell, Lawrence. Maybe you gone and done him a favor. Poor coot." The two men looked down on George. Lefty called to his night guards, who were also volunteer militia men in this far-flung American settlement. "Take care of the body. And close his mouth and eyes, for God's sake," Lefty barked. "When you're done, you better ride up to Aurora in the morning. Get there before too many days pass and notify the Rifles there what happened. Ask for extra men to be sent this way. We're going to need protection, boys. They'll attack soon as word gets to them that their George is killed."

Lawrence Jones, on the advice of Lefty, stayed inside the barn with the two armed men stationed outside. He rested atop an army cot, lying on his back, staring at the wooden beams and listening closely to rats moving in and out of food stores. He did not fall asleep. He imagined every twig that cracked and each coyote's step as an Indian chief approaching. He pulled the blanket tighter around his body and covered his eyes with it. Somehow, what you can't see is less powerful when underneath the wool. He blew hot breath into the rough fibers of the blanket to ward off the barn's stiffening, unforgiving air, the cold as oppressive as humid summers in Carthage and just as full of discomfort.

Lefty worried too. He moved Lawrence as far from the house and his wife as he could while still providing protection to his employee. "Goddamned hothead," he muttered to himself as he loaded his rifle. He cleaned his gun and kept an eye on the barn and the distant borders of his ranch.

The next day, Lawrence volunteered to ride with the night guards, thinking it best to help the reinforcement efforts against the Paiute that he had precipitated. He had slept only after dawn broke, his breath flowing normally after a fitful night listening to branches brushing the windows and vermin racing through the barn's eaves.

On the trail, sagebrush chipmunks and mountain cottontail rabbits spooked the horses, prompting one of the guards to remark that something just wasn't right, that they all ought to be on the lookout.

"I got a feeling, boys," one of the guards said. An hour passed. Lawrence Jones' eyelids dipped of their own accord, and his chin rested on his chest. His horse sidestepped volcanic rocks and silver miners' rubbish—broken pickaxes, tin pans beset by bullet holes, frayed wool socks, and empty bean and tomato cans. Lawrence felt the weight of his head and suddenly jerked awake. He yawned. A thick snowfall adhered to the valley floor. Lawrence pulled his coat tighter around his neck and adjusted his hat. But after a few minutes, he was unable to resist sleep. It came despite the dense flakes and weak sunlight. Then he saw it. The coyote.

Coyote, who panted as if fresh from pursuit of his dinner, fixed his eyes on Lawrence Jones. The coyote whispered in man's language: "The battle will begin. You have angered the chief." But Lawrence did not believe in animals speaking, even in a dream, so he quickly shook his head, took stock of his horse's steps, and called to the man in front for the distance left to ride. "About halfway," the guard said.

Lawrence realized he had not eaten since noon the previous day. Remembering the small satchel that the cook had tied to his saddle, Lawrence unraveled its contents and set about eating corn bread with butter. The snow abruptly halted and the sky was clearing. He looked up after finishing his small but satisfying meal and did not see either guard. *I've fallen a bit behind,* he thought, but he did not worry since he could hear the bits inside their horses' mouths chiming against the metal rein hooks. Lawrence smiled. He was happy. The West was made for men like him—risk-takers with lightning reflexes and a willingness to stake a claim and wake the land from its wasteful slumber. He took a deep breath, yawned, and unknowingly closed his eyes.

Lawrence Jones spotted a large, handsome steer branded with Lefty's mark not twenty paces from where his horse plodded along the trail. *What is that steer doing so far from the ranch?* He recognized the steer, but why? *Why did the dang Hereford remind him of something?* He rubbed his eyes. A boy suddenly appeared, walking alongside the red-brown Hereford. The boy's right hand rested on the steer's neck. *The dumb Indian? Impossible! He was dead! He was buried!* Lawrence questioned the day, the passing storm, the horse he rode, who was now jumpy and disobedient. Lawrence did not believe in ghosts, in an afterlife, in visions or dreams. And since he did not believe in what he saw, he chose to look away, unscrew the cap from his canteen, and pour water over his face.

"Having a hard time staying awake there, Jones?" the guard behind him asked, riding so close that his horse's snout touched the tail of Lawrence's horse. Lawrence jumped.

"Where did you come from?"

"Been riding right behind you all along," the guard said. Lawrence turned to offer his canteen.

"No, no, I got plenty myself. I don't get thirsty in this cold," the guard said. "You keep that water for yourself. You're going to need it. Got a ways to go just yet."

"You see a steer and a boy walking next to it?"

The guard answered, much to Lawrence's relief, "No, ain't seen nothing and nobody since we left. Don't typically see any cattle this way. Maybe a miner now and then. You new around here?"

"Yes, just started working for Lefty about a month ago. Came from Carthage, Illinois, originally."

"This place ain't nothing like where you are from, is it?" the guard asked.

All was suddenly silent, the horses' hooves made no sound, crows ceased their staccato calls, and rabbits hopped noiselessly between the rocks and brush. Lawrence looked at the sky, expecting thick, ink-colored clouds or impending lightning to explain the quiet that had overcome the land so quickly. He slapped the palm of his hand against his head. *Maybe my hearing's going,* he thought, *or worse, my mind.*

Up ahead, the first guard shouted "Indians!" An arrow missed Lawrence and his horse's head by an uncomfortable margin. The arrow did not seem as weak or as bad as he had heard from the other ranch hands around Lefty's. He ducked, clutched the reins, and gave a fierce series of kicks to his horse. The second guard pulled his rifle from across his chest and aimed toward large boulders where a band of

Paiutes on foot had arrayed themselves. The horses, now uncontrollable, ran off the trail toward a ravine with a small dry creek bed. Lawrence struggled to gather up the reins, which had fallen from his grip. He looked frantically for Indians on either side and managed to remove his revolver from his hip. His horse followed the first guard's closely. Another arrow was loosed upon Lawrence, and it came closer to its intended resting point. Lawrence slumped forward onto the horse's neck, tasting the coarse, long strands of salty mane in his mouth. He raised his head, quickly surveyed his body, and concluded he had not been hit. He looked ahead and realized the guard in front had fallen out of the saddle. Lawrence turned and saw the guard on the ground, an arrow firmly planted in his chest. He wondered if he should turn around, but the second man rode closely behind, spurring all of the horses onward.

When Lawrence, the remaining guard, and the horse with the empty saddle arrived in Aurora, the miners had already come into town for their supper. Main Street was busy and no one paid attention to the two men. Lawrence and the guard walked into the Tunnel Saloon, where their soiled clothing and unshaven faces went unremarked. The guard bought Lawrence two whiskeys and three for himself. Then they proceeded to the Wingate Building to see about the Rifles, the Esmeralda Rangers' militia. Lawrence let the guard do all the talking. He didn't pay close attention, but he heard the guard say "Lefty's employee," "killed down the gully a few miles west," and "no end to what they'll do."

The Rifles man turned to Lawrence and the night guard. "Well, what's Lefty's man getting killed for?"

"Sometimes there's no reason," the guard said. But since there was one, Lawrence spoke up.

"Even the score. I killed an Indian that was stealing one of Lefty's cows."

"I see. It's time to show these Indians a thing or two. Get washed up, gentlemen. Join the Rifles for supper. Twenty-five cents at Harkness' place will get you a meal." He waved Lawrence and the guard toward the back where some women in loose-fitting cottons delivered a steady supply of hot water.

After his bath, Lawrence walked to Pine Street, feeling renewed and optimistic that this whole Indian business would get resolved and the people would be protected. He fancied himself playing the part of civilian soldier who would prepare a battle plan and win a hero's welcome back in the valley. He stopped short of Harkness' and set aside his thoughts on the Indian problem when he saw a dozen men in a strange fervor gathered around what appeared to be a small animal skin. It was no animal. A lantern's light cast diabolical shadows on skin and hair coated in dried blood. It was the scalp of Lefty's dead guard. No man dared touch the thing.

"Beasts," one of the men said. "They've the heart of lions. Revenge, they have got to have it, and more to come too, I bet."

"But they're stealing *our* property, and they've got to

know that isn't right," Lawrence said. His voice cracked. The Esmeralda Rangers exchanged knowing glances.

"You're not talking about regular people here," the man said. "They like to dance over the scalps. Not this time. We're facing a race that hasn't never had the rule of law. But I tell you one thing. Some of them are intelligent. May be Indians, but some of them's got minds, sharp minds."

After dinner, the company began drinking gin and smoking Havana cigars at Porter's. These amusements seemed to relieve, for Lawrence anyway, the memory of the dead guard and postpone the dread that would settle in as the skies dimmed. In the distance, a coyote called. Lawrence looked up, his breath now short and his palms watery. A man slapped him on the back.

"You jumpy, Mr. Jones? Don't worry, nothing is gonna happen here in Aurora. Coyote is a problem in the Indian stories, but he isn't gonna come after you. In their tales, Coyote is always trying to take something that don't belong to him. He's a troublemaker, and because he's clever, he survives. A considerable creature, if you ask me," the man added as he poured himself more Old Tom Holland's.

Eventually, Lawrence retired to his cot to get some sleep. But he tossed and turned, waking early in the morning to seek his blanket, which he had torn off in his fitful sleep. He sat up, recalling a fragment of a dream in which a coyote with lustrous fur instructed him to follow a reedy but imposing Indian. His head throbbed from the gin. *I am a no-account fool,* he thought. He leaned back on the cot and closed his eyes, listening to the twitters of quail as they sought their breakfast just outside the window.

Soon, his dreaming returned, and Lawrence was powerless to stop its course. He found himself walking along the Owens River where Lefty's cattle had worn a path among the cattails. They had trammeled the wild heliotrope's pale blue petals, which had not yet learned to take shelter among hardier plants. The flow of the brown water, full of small fish darting through the lazy current, reflected Lawrence's lanky frame. Just ahead of Lawrence walked a wide-shouldered Indian and a small boy. Lawrence was unafraid, curious even, so he picked up his pace to catch up and present himself. The young Indian spoke first.

"This is my father, the Irrigator," he said in English. The boy's fingers flicked against each other and fluttered up from his sides, as animated as butterfly wings after weeks in a tight cocoon.

"Hello, I am Lawrence," he answered in an unknown tongue.

"You speak our language," the father said. "You will help us to build a small ditch? We need to water our crops."

"I will help," Lawrence said. "But where are your crops?"

"Seeds and tubers, just that way," the Irrigator replied.

"Can men live on that alone?"

"Father is the chosen man to water the fields this year. Our food store is small, but with blessings from rain and the river, it is enough for all of us to eat," the young boy said, his teeth bright as dried bones. The sun warmed their chests as they walked.

"I know a thing or two about ditches," Lawrence began. "I'm Mormon. We practically invented farming in the desert. Let me walk with you. I will dig a beautiful ditch and keep it clear of weeds." The boy smiled and the tall father nodded.

A rooster crowed before sunrise, waking Lawrence, who was weary from the dreams, the visions, the animals, and the Indians who visited despite his protests. *I must get some real sleep,* he thought, rising to pack his saddlebag to return to the ranch and one of the small bunkhouse beds at Lefty's.

The detachment rode along Pine Street as the sun began to rise. Lawrence's eyes were swollen and he yawned repeatedly, never seeming able to take in a full gulp of air. His appetite for vengeance seemed to have decreased, and he looked at the other men for a sign of their commitment to this new battle. He shook his head, hoping that the treacherous thoughts that clouded his mind would disintegrate and fall away. Surely the lack of sleep and uneasy dreams were contributing to his doubts? Of course he would kill Indians today, and of course he belonged in this detachment as a proud employee of Lefty McAuliffe and his cattle ranch. He picked the yellow crust from the corners of his eyes and emptied water from his canteen straight into his throat.

As the detachment neared Lefty's, a scout cried out that Indians were approaching on foot.

"One of them is Shoandow," the scout said. "Don't got

27

into nothing with us before but keep your guard up. You never know."

Lawrence got a long look at what appeared to be a trustworthy Indian. But hadn't Lawrence's mother told him not to trust nobody in the West, that scoundrels and thieves looked charming at every glance? Lawrence wondered if the Esmeralda Rangers would shoot now or later. Some of the militia men seemed to know Shoandow and lowered their rifles.

"This is an Indian we can do business with," the scout said under his breath.

Shoandow spoke first. "I come to tell you that I am here to recover a colt, a mare, and one with red color and white whiskers."

"You here to say your horses been stolen?" the Ranger asked.

"Yes, I regret to say. Stolen last night while we slept in the rocks." Shoandow's face nodded toward the slough bordered by the tablelands.

"You leave your weapons here, Chief, and we'll let you pass by to go about seeing where your horses have gotten off to. Suspect they ran off in the night."

"Didn't run off, sir. Stolen."

"Well, it could have been miners up in Benton," the Ranger said.

"We will go now," Shoandow said.

"You will lay down your guns," the Ranger said sternly. "Your people will not kill any more of ours."

"But we need protection. Just as you. You killed one of our sons, the boy you called George," Shoandow said. Lawrence held his breath. One of the braves behind Shoandow moved his left hand toward his otter skin quiver. A Rifle's horse moved anxiously, tapping its hooves and swishing its tail. Then the Ranger fired. Shoandow fell back like timber being cut in an alpine meadow, slow and graceful. Lawrence's horse bucked, let out an alarmed high-pitched cry, and circled on itself before charging away from the trail. Under a rainstorm of Indian arrows, the horse was full of terror. Lawrence bounced hard in the saddle, his boots having slipped from the stirrups and his hands unable to catch onto the reins, which had fallen around the horse's ears. He bent down to embrace the horse's neck in hopes that his own hair would miraculously blend into the horse's mane and that perhaps his entire body would fuse with the horse's ample chest and shoulders, long legs, and tufted fetlocks.

An Indian loosed an arrow that grazed the horse's rump. Though the horse had felt more irritation from a gnat or a fly, he leaped and wheeled on his haunches, possessed of a furious energy and demonic determination, and when his front hooves hit the ground, Lawrence saw that he was not fleeing from certain death, but galloping headlong into it. The reins remained just out of reach. With a better view, the Indian hit Lawrence with ease, and the Indian's obsidian point lodged itself underneath Lawrence's skin and burned into the flesh between his bottom-most ribs on his left side.

Lawrence squinted and gripped the moist mane, unable to control the horse, whose mouth tossed back copious drops of froth that landed in Lawrence's eyes. The arrow, erratic as it bounced between Lawrence's rib cage and the horse's neck, succumbed to the commotion, its shaft eventually breaking off inside the wound.

Lawrence closed his eyes and said a prayer, but not the kind of prayer his mother said with him before bed so many years ago. It seemed to come through him from a glacial bellows up above, a vast current of stony air flapping its course through his blood. He looked up and saw wings, wings so enormous they blocked out the sun's rays. He could make out a hooked beak and a white-crowned head. Surely this was a trick from the Indian obsidian? Then he heard the eagle.

"Brother, they are all dead. Return to your home. Let this battle be done and the summer begin. Let this insufferable winter end and the people be fed. Return home, young brother, they are all dead."

The horse stopped its terrifying gallop, yanked its head in the direction of Mount Tom, and started off again at breakneck speed. Lawrence felt the point bury itself farther into his body. Lefty's ranch neared and the horse, exhausted as it was, kept a steady pace, its eyes still enlarged and wild, its nostrils flared and straining to take in enough air.

When they arrived, the horse stopped without command. Lawrence dismounted and led it into the corral near the bunkhouse, making sure to fill the water trough and leave a pile of fresh hay for the spent animal. He then walked absently to his bed. The other ranch hands were still out in the valley, and for this he was glad. He desired only to sleep, not caring to administer to his wound or report on the events.

When Lawrence woke several hours later to the silence of the valley darkness, he felt strangely elated, his limbs tingling with a careless joy and his eyes freshly seeing despite the black veil of the hour. Lawrence rose, tucked in his wool shirt, placed his hat on top of his head, and pushed the door. He walked past the corral, past the barn, around the McAuliffe home, and out a wooden gate to the cottonwood-lined road. He walked down through the valley until he reached the cliffs of the volcanic tableland. He found a narrow trail that mounted the ancient ash flow, up the steep-sloped wall covered with fine pale sand and rocks. He climbed, undeterred by the difficult soil into which his boots sank, eyeing the way so suddenly illuminated by the moon. He touched his side from time to time as if to search for something he had lost.

When he reached the top, he turned. No one stirred in the bunkhouse below. The land seemed to be taking a giant breath, suspended between night and day. Then, emerging from the cottonwoods, a procession: a steer, a young Paiute, and a coyote. Flying closely behind, a bird. Lawrence did not shake his head this time or blame the vision on his fatigued state. The young man below stopped, turned toward the uplifted earth where Lawrence was perched, and held his hand above his head, revealing fingers dancing in the moon's shower of light, fingers climbing an invisible ladder, gesturing to the top of the tablelands. Lawrence stood, raised his own arm, and nodded toward the animals and the Indian. The Indian turned back to the south and walked alone, his companions' heads lowered in respect and assent as he left the valley.

Lawrence was overcome with a sudden pain in his side and fell to the sandy cap of the scarp. Fatigue descended on his chest. He rolled onto his back, comfortable if only because he had not slept well for many nights and any place would do.

He slipped into a dream, following the Indian all night and half the next day, all the way to Owens Lake, which had not yet dried up. Birds called to one another as they pounced on the lake's abundance. Their cacophony replaced the sound of his heart, their flapping bodies blanketing the water so that Lawrence was unsure if a lake actually pooled beneath their gathered feathers, claws, and beaks. Lawrence wanted to find the Indian, but the birds were too numerous and made too much noise. He bent over and placed his finger in the water, touching what had once been snow before it made its alpine to desert valley journey. The air turned quiet and the birds flew up toward the mountains. He sat on the edge of the lake and listened to the howls of distant coyotes and the calls of an eagle. Their plaintive sounds filled the valley from west to east, from the jagged and snowy peaks to the rounded copper hills and ancient volcanic cones. They echoed from the miners' claims all the way to the bristlecone trees, which listened from their sentry posts in the rain shadow, their boughs bending imperceptibly in unified comprehension.

Life would be different for everyone—man, river, tree, lake, steer, coyote, and eagle. All would be changed. All were changing, the trees said, adding that it had always been so. The Indian was gone. Lawrence wondered if he had drowned in the lake's endless waters.

The dream ended, and Lawrence gratefully slept unmolested atop the salmon-colored tableland until the sun shone harshly on his beaten frame. When he awoke, he adjusted his hat and took a stilted breath.

The obsidian point remained between his ribs, coming ever so close to puncturing the sac of breath and the cage of one beat up, but still beating, heart. It never did. Every now and then, a small amount of pain sprung from his side, but Lawrence Jones did not complain. He would stand for a few moments and look across to the cliffs topped by a pink spine, summoning the Indian, the cow, the coyote, and the eagle. They always came, but their appearance was quickly followed by a dusty swirl of sand. After many years, Lawrence realized no one else would or could catch him in this act of seeing what could not be seen. "The wind's whipping up on that ridge," Lawrence would say to Lefty, and always Lefty replied, "Why, sure is."

That morning on the scarp, Lawrence Jones lowered himself down the slope and went back to Lefty's ranch and the Hereford cattle, back to the possibilities of this new frontier, back to the battles that would be fought to bring more men to the valley. He thought only of his thirst and hunger and hoped that the cook would be up and have the coffee on the stove and some bacon frying in his iron skillet. For now, it was easier to think of breakfast.

What Is Rightly Mine

"I believe we will be millionaires," the Reverend said to Aunt Sturdy, who adjusted her eyeglasses, peered at the religious man and his companion, and, in that moment, held two opposing thoughts at once—that she had always been a good Christian and that she would have that money. Aunt Sturdy's border collie, drowsy from the afternoon heat, looked up briefly, his place on the covered, wooden-plank porch of the Profit Inn of Aurora the coolest he could find.

She took their hands in hers. Aunt Sturdy noticed the religious man's smooth, relatively unscathed knuckles. "This is my good friend Samuel," he said. Samuel's hands were rough, calloused, and dry.

"So you hit a vein?" Aunt Sturdy asked. The miner Samuel nodded.

"Lady Luck, ma'am. We aim to stake a claim nearby. My friend here won't keep the money, of course, but might build a parish. Lots of men are forgetting God."

"And you, Mr. Samuel?" Aunt Sturdy wanted to know what the miner had planned.

"Oh, I don't know, ma'am. Never expected to strike it rich. I do know I'd like to buy my friend a drink if you've got one. A celebration is in order."

"Well," Aunt Sturdy said brightly, "a celebration we will have. I've got a nice cut of beef, some fresh fruit from the orchards in the valley, and a well-stocked cabinet. I'll go and prepare your room." She bounded up the stairs of the Profit Inn and busied herself with making the beds and filling two vases with dried lupines and irises. The purple shades of the flowers filled her with optimism. She changed the linens and unwrapped a bar of soap. The men might like to shave, she thought, so she pulled her deceased husband's razors and brushes from the medicine cabinet and lined them up neatly on the white coverlet of the bed.

Aunt Sturdy accepted the men's invitation to sit for a drink. "But first I'll get supper going. I have a girl who's real good, and all I need to do is give her the orders. I'm not much for whiskey, so I'll just boil the coffee. I admit I would like to hear your story. Got so many mirages out there—stream-beds that yield nothing but rubble and disappointment."

"And you'll need to tell us how you got your name, if you don't mind, Aunt Sturdy," Samuel said.

"It's a short story," Aunt Sturdy said. "My husband's name was Walter Sturdy. I guess I got the name Aunt from the miners. I'm old enough to be their mothers, but they was being polite by calling me Aunt instead. And I took care of many an injured miner. Mostly I saved them but sometimes the loss of blood was too great. I do my best and I keep a clean inn and cook good meals. Guess that's the best thing I can do in these times." She turned to the kitchen, light in her cheerful girth, and soon returned with ample drink for Samuel and the Reverend.

"Now, let's hear your tale, gentlemen," she said, placing a tumbler in front of each man and pouring generous ounces of whiskey. *I want them to really talk*, she thought.

"We came, like the others came, for fortune and adventure. The Reverend here came to pay particular attention to the miners and their families, their social and moral state of affairs. As for me, I've just been hired by an outfit in Virginia City that wants me to describe this whole enterprise. I endeavor to relate these capers for an audience willing to read them. Meanwhile," Samuel continued, "we've had our eye on what was coming out of the World West shaft. You saw how crazed the district has been, all kinds of people saying they had struck it rich. Well, the World West shaft was yielding specimens of soft rock with bits of gold and even bigger bits of silver. When you washed it, it gleaned so brightly. You know, World West had offers from investors all over. Some were offering thousands of dollars per foot, but none of them was accepted."

"So what did World West do?" Aunt Sturdy asked.

"They did what a smart company would do and put a stop to the hauling away of the specimens," the Reverend said. "I may be a holy man, but I took a good long look at what specimens were coming out of that shaft. I suspected right away they weren't from the World West vein."

"He said to me three nights ago, 'Couldn't be World West rock! I'm going to go down the shaft and prove it,'" Samuel said.

"And I did. I waited and waited for the watchmen to go off duty," the Reverend said.

"He had to drop down and lie in wait like a mountain lion hunting a bighorn. He stayed that way for hours but finally crawled to the opening of the shaft, looked about for the guards, and grabbed the rope. Slid down until he was surrounded by the gloom. About that time, one of the guards returned and called down. But the Reverend was quiet and quick as a lizard, not making any noise and certainly not answering the call. Eventually, the guard gave up and left him down there," Samuel said.

"So I was down there, letting my eyes adjust, and I saw what I had predicted—a blind lead," the Reverend said.

"A blind lead! What luck! I shall drink to that," Aunt Sturdy said, pouring a dash of whiskey in her coffee and gulping with delight. "But what about the World West Company? Don't they know about the lead?"

"Not as far as I can tell. Their rock is different. It's easy to tell the difference once you've been around the rock for a good while. It is the public's property. The lead's inside its own rocks and clay, cutting its way through the World West vein. Aunt Sturdy, it's ours!" Samuel said, pouring more drink and patting the Reverend on the back.

"Just think what the Reverend here could do with such money. He could erect his church, a hospital, all for the civic betterment," Samuel said.

"It's a dream for me. I came west to help men, and now the good Lord is helping me to do just that."

"What happens next then?" Aunt Sturdy asked.

"Well, that's why we've come here," the Reverend said.

"What do you mean?" said Aunt Sturdy.

"Well, Aunt Sturdy, you have a relation, we understand, who's working for the foreman at World West."

"I was afraid you'd ask me about that."

"We aren't going to ask you to do anything you're not bent on doing," the Reverend said.

"What we would like for you to consider is to invite your relation—he's your nephew, isn't he? Invite him to meet with us here. We would like to ask him to help us take ownership of the blind lead. That way, we can record it and establish ourselves as owners. We'll take him down to show him proof that it doesn't belong to World West. Then we'll ask him to go in on it together, each person getting one-fourth," Samuel explained.

"Divide the earnings into fourths? Who is the fourth?" Aunt Sturdy asked.

"Why, we would like to propose that it's you, ma'am," the Reverend said.

"I don't know what to say! I am overcome." Aunt Sturdy's eyes welled and her cheeks reddened with excitement. She recalled a time long ago when she, a girl servant in an Army captain's home full of beautiful daughters with ample choices, prepared their Parisian dresses, which would go on to make appearances in drawing rooms all over Manhattan. She had never once received any compliment about her looks nor suitability for marriage. For the first time, she was being courted. "I cannot say no. It's too good to be true!"

"But it's true indeed, Aunt Sturdy," Samuel said.

"I saw it with my own eyes," the Reverend said.

"Gentlemen, this spring day is still new and I've a wonderful idea. Ever been out on the Mono Lake in a boat?"

"No, ma'am, that lake seems lifeless and bleak," said the Reverend.

"It's full of life, gentlemen. Come, I'll row you out, and we can picnic and enjoy our good fortune."

Aunt Sturdy assembled the repast, issuing clipped, no-nonsense orders to her cook girl. Then the kitchen went quiet, though a distinctly hushed conversation could be detected. The Reverend and Samuel did not take any pains to discern its meaning.

The merry party set out on horses for the thirty-five-mile journey from Aurora to a makeshift dock on Mono Lake where several rowboats tied to salty posts awaited. Mrs. Sturdy paid a shifty, skinny boy for the boat and for watering and feeding their horses. Aunt Sturdy insisted on rowing despite Samuel's protestations.

Her strength was impressive. She rowed toward the islands in the lake.

"Is there enough time to reach them and return in the daylight?" the Reverend asked.

"Sure is. Won't be a storm tonight. The water is like glass, and if I get tired, I'll ask one of you to row," Aunt Sturdy said. Samuel was elated.

"This will be in the book too! What a grand adventure. I'm speechless," he said.

"Surprising for you, my young, loquacious friend," the Reverend said, laughing and lighting a pipe.

"What will you do with your money, Aunt Sturdy?" Samuel asked.

"I will go to San Francisco and buy a mansion high above the bay. I will order the best dresses from Europe and eat meat every day. I want to finally be part of the new society. I will attend the opera and ballet," she said, smiling and continuing to row with gumption and speed.

Late in the day they landed on the black island.

"It's hideous if you ask me," Samuel said. "Haven't felt so lonely as being here makes me feel."

"Oh, Samuel, you're just not seeing with proper eyes. It's a magnificent place once you get to know it," Aunt Sturdy said. The three walked ashore with a satchel of victuals and whiskey. Aunt Sturdy wiped the sweat from her face and neck. "This place is like no other. I am awestruck each time I see the fantastical towers shooting out of the water with osprey nests atop their spires. Look at the seagull colony on the island! Seems simple—the flies feed on the invisible food of the lake, the birds feed on the flies, and millions, I mean just more than one could ever count, millions of birds arrive. I run my inn for the miners, but this lake runs her own inn for the animals. They receive enough food and rest to raise their children. And then they leave. I feel awfully sad to see them go, but it's in the natural order of things. It's a grand lake—a salty sea in a desert ringed by mountains. Even the most fruitful imagination couldn't conjure such a sight. You must write about it in your book, Samuel," Aunt Sturdy said.

"America's Dead Sea," Samuel said. "But I can't say I care for it. The crooked, lumpy pumice-stone towers and the gray, sluggish water so strong with salt. It's all a bit curious. I, for one, would not want to get stranded."

"Well, we'll just have to disagree on your assessment," Aunt Sturdy said.

"Fine. I never disagree on disagreement," Samuel said.

"I'll spread this blanket and we can have a nice drink," Aunt Sturdy said. As the afternoon wore on, she watched her charges indulge in the whiskey. She merely sipped at her own, letting it wash in and out of her mouth and back into the glass.

"Well, gentlemen, if you don't mind, I've got to relieve myself. I'll be just a few moments." Aunt Sturdy disappeared over the rise of the island's highest point and descended toward a path that wound around to the boat. She arrived several minutes later, out of breath but with plenty of energy left. She settled in the boat, grabbed the oars, and pushed against the soft shore. The sun was now completely hidden behind the mountains and only twilight remained. Overhead, thunderclouds were forming. *They'll be just fine, those two,* she thought. *I left them with some canvas for cover and plenty of bread.* She turned to see the two silhouettes that were now standing and looking about. *They'll get worried in a few minutes and set off in search for me. But for a little while longer, they'll just assume I'm still off taking my leave.*

She rowed with ever more power and speed as the island receded and the small dock came into view. At its edge stood Aunt Sturdy's kitchen girl.

"Don't just stand there. Help me out of this contraption!" The girl had grown used to her barked commands, as they often meant that a miner was hurt and emergency attention was required.

Aunt Sturdy rode beside her employee, who drove the horse on with a small whip. The wind blew the girl's shawl to the ground, and she looked to see if she ought to stop, but Aunt Sturdy's look told her it would be a very bad idea indeed.

Back on the island, the men dithered about whether Aunt Sturdy was returning. They argued about what constituted a reasonable amount of time for a woman to perform the aforementioned duties of relief. Once they agreed she had abandoned them to their own devices, they discussed how to get back to shore.

"I'll jump in. It's not so deep, is it?" Samuel asked.

"Not the depth you should worry about. It's the size of the waves, it's the salt that will sting your eyes and tear your clothes asunder."

"I'll wear my glasses, I'll swim fast—I won the Nevada state championship, you know. I'm a fine swimmer," Samuel said.

"Don't doubt it. But what are you proposing? To swim back to shore and fetch a boat, meanwhile leaving me alone?"

"No, guess I don't want to do that."

"I'm scared of the dark, son."

"But you've got God to protect you, Reverend. And you've been in the deepest mines."

"This dark isn't the same."

"You're right. It's awful menacing on this island."

"With you here, I stand a chance of making it. We can huddle for warmth until daybreak. Surely the woman will send a boat."

"She'll leave us here until she can claim the lead for herself."

"Well, even if that were so, you couldn't catch her at this point."

Samuel nodded, sat at the edge of the fire, and chewed off a large portion of stale bread. The whiskey was nearly done. "Here, Reverend, go ahead and take the last of it."

"Don't mind if I do," the Reverend said.

Samuel waited until the Reverend had fallen asleep. Samuel stood up. The whitecaps grew to at least three feet in height. *I am not the state champion for nothing,* he thought. He waded into the cold water, which immediately stung all of the scratches and sores on his legs and arms. *It's cleansing me. I can't let it stop me. I will claim that blind lead. She doesn't know exactly where to look. There's still time. I can reach the shore in an hour's time. I will do it. For the Reverend, for myself. I will be rich. No one will take that away from me. Not a conniving dog of a woman. No, she will not win this game.* Samuel dipped his hands into the water, sharp as a razor's edge on his skin.

He kept a steady pace with his head raised, but the wind increased, and soon conditions necessitated closing his eyes and letting the waves wash over his body. He sucked gulps of air, as much as he could, hoping the storm would not worsen. Despite his efforts to keep his head out of the salty stew, after several minutes he could no longer see. He couldn't turn back, for where was back? And he hardly knew the way forward, so he just prayed, a quiet simple prayer: *By your grace, return me to town so that what is mine will not be stolen.*

The wind whipped ever higher, the waves becoming unruly and pushing Samuel off course. His eyes filled with tears, and the salt confronted him with persistent needles of pain. He took a breath, saw that the moon was rising, and momentarily listened to the birds gathering from the west. *I'll float on my back a few minutes, just rest a bit before opening these stinging eyes,* he thought. But a gust of wind, so bitter and fierce, arose, pulling his body under. Against his better judgment, he opened his eyes. Where was the surface? There was no discerning the sky from the vast lake bottom as swarms of miniature shrimp clouded the water. He closed his eyes and kicked. Could he reach the surface? He did not know where the surface was. Could he make a guess and a go of it? Would he live? The blind lead was no longer on his mind. Only the sky. If he could see the sky. If he could see a star, any star, or see the moon above. If only.

Samuel wanted nothing more than to open his mouth, his eyes, to take a breath. Nothing was more important. Nothing. Not eating, drinking, sleeping, loving a woman. Nothing. Only breath. Air. Without air he was nothing. His chest hardened. He started to sink, his chin now touching his chest. Was he giving up? He thought about what that meant and shook his head at the thought of having the leisure to contemplate the ever after. Then he fell asleep, a long, deeply satisfying sleep full of luxurious dreams in which he laughed, breathing in fragrant air saturated with the calls of the gulls gathering. As he sank deeper, he saw orange poppies lining the road to the lake and the rabbit brush coming into bloom. The Reverend walked a path just above the tent camps, an elegant walking stick in his hand. Samuel plucked the poppies, dozens of them, eager to make a wild bouquet. He chose hyacinth and the mountain for-get-me-nots and tied them with a piece of twine. He walked to the Profit Inn and asked the girl to give the flowers to Aunt Sturdy. "Give them to her yourself," she said. Aunt Sturdy appeared. "Don't mind my clothes," Samuel said.

"They've all but disintegrated after my swim in the lake," he added. Aunt Sturdy laughed and invited him in. "One of the guests left behind his trousers and a work shirt. I've laundered them and you are welcome to them," she said, turning to mount the stairs as she wiped her hands on her apron. "Been baking all morning. I hope you'll join me for some tea and biscuits."

Suddenly the dream ends. Samuel touches his face. It is so wet and sharp pins are being inserted everywhere. He wants to shout "Help me! Help me!" But there is no air. Still, he attempts to take a much-needed breath. *If I do not breathe, I shall not exist.* Even if there is no air to be found down here. He pushes off a tufa rock tower, bubbles rising from the deep. Looking up, Samuel sees a shining beacon. It is the moon and he will touch it. But he has lost his strength; he cannot move his arms or feet. He knows the surface is near. His mind is blank, his eyes see only the moon. Then, nothing. Darkness.

But the birds have come. A dozen eared grebes are grasping Samuel's tattered wool trousers and shirt in their beaks. Some have taken hold of Samuel's boot strings. The small birds, together, are tugging the man upward. Some are merely flying under his armpits and behind his back, leaning their empty bones into his dense ones and powering their feet in haste. In just a few moments, the birds have propelled Samuel to the surface. He chokes and the inhalation mixes with the regurgitated water. He attempts to breathe and exhale and remove the water from his stomach all at the same time. Then Samuel notices the moon. It's rounder than a china plate, and on its surface are valleys and canyons glowing amber and copper. There are stars too, numerous and close, silver nuggets in a bag of black rock. *I am rich,* he thinks. *I am one of the richest men in the West. I have claimed the blind lead, and the silver's been picked away.* He takes a deeper breath and then expels more salty water and the evening's libations. *Truly I am a celebrated man. I will do good now that I am a man of wealth, now that I have made my mark and taken what is most rightly mine.*

The diving grebes take their leave of Samuel. A gentle wave has brought the miner ashore. The winds have paused in their wrath, unable to sustain their assault, and for now they settle in the nearby volcanic cones and hills. The night's thick with the sounds of birds—gulls, phalaropes, diving ducks, ospreys, and hawks calling to their kin, to their neighbors to the north, to the bears in the lands of departed glaciers, to the fish in the rivers. All is safe, if not for long, at least in this moment. And animals, it is well known, live for the minute in which their hearts beat, not for the millions of heartbeats to come.

Samuel's heart beat gladly anew. As he slowly regained his composure, a night watchman from a nearby ranch stopped and asked if Samuel had "killed his man?" Not hearing a reply, the watchman slung Samuel over the front of his horse and took him back to where the matron could minister to him, for surely only a victor in a cold-blooded, murderous battle would find himself on the shores of

desolate Mono Lake in the middle of the night. And anyways, he was bored and looked forward to the man's tale.
Someone was always getting killed or doing the killing in
this part of the world. He urged his horse on to Aurora.

The Reverend did not often pray for himself, but as the
fire died down, he pulled a wool blanket around his shoulders and tucked his chin into his chest. *Dear Lord, lend your
protective hand to this task of survival, to my dear friend
Samuel, to the sinner Mrs. Sturdy, to all who search for sal-
vation in this barren land. Give me strength and clarity, send
me your courage—and in return you will have my ever loving
devotion, hundred-fold more than you have had until now. I
will promise to serve you in this lake devoid of life and this
land so full of temptation. I will work on your behalf to bring
the sinners to the table of your holy bounty. Spare me, Lord.
Give me one more day and one more night.*

He felt the wind picking up and wondered if Samuel
was indeed as strong a swimmer as he claimed. He was
alone on this black island, the fire dead, the night turning all about his head, a rescue boat nowhere in sight. The
Reverend chewed on a question: *Does God hear one man?*
Then he saw a flock of gulls. *Odd for this time of night.
Where are they going?* He stared into the void. Behind the
hills capped with sloping, washbasin-like depressions, the
full moon had begun its ascent, bathing the Reverend in
cool but reassuring light, illuminating the birds as they
alighted on the island opposite. He was no longer alone. The
gulls settled into comfortable postures, quietly assembling

themselves, fluffing out their feathers against the cool air. The time to lay their eggs had come. New life would emerge in the coming days, the Reverend thought. He was comforted by their presence, their murmurings to one another, their bright-white softness lit by the moon. *Does God hear one man?* Perhaps. *The birds were sent, surely they were sent to accompany me,* he thought. A night has interminable length with only thoughts, one's own wicked, wondering thoughts, for companions.

Aunt Sturdy and the girl arrived at World West. Campfires burned brightly, the sparks distinct and blowing freely in the wind. Laughter and grunting came from her nephew Stewart's cabin. Aunt Sturdy turned to the girl, who shrugged.

"Guess I'll be interrupting a little party," Aunt Sturdy said, straightening her apron and flattening the fabric against her ample chest. She bellowed Stewart's name so that the men and women in all of the nearby cabins went dead silent. Stewart appeared at the opening, grinning, his chin glistening with chicken fat and his breath stinking of gin.

"Aunt Sturdy, what a surprise," he said, wiping a streak from the corner of his mouth with the back of his hand. "I'd invite you to come inside out of the night, but I got company." A woman inside yelled "Git back here!" to Stewart.

"I got to go, Aunt Sturdy. Real nice seeing you. And you too," he said, removing an invisible hat and bowing to the women.

"Now Stewart, I don't rightly care you got yourself a woman in violation of the Lord's instructions, but look here. I got to talk to you right away."

"As you wish, Aunt Sturdy, but can it wait until morning?"

She shook her head. "Now, Stewart, you must talk to me now! If not, we'll both be a lot less richer."

"Funny you should mention that, Aunt Sturdy. I'm already plenty rich."

"Well, what I have to say will make us both wealthy beyond our dreams. I will finally have that house in San Francisco. I will have all that I want, and you too, you will be able to retire, to settle down with a nice girl, not like the ones you have here. Oh, nephew, don't you see? All our troubles will be gone!" Aunt Sturdy's eyes shone with tears of possibility.

"Aunt Sturdy, I told you. I am already very rich. Not an hour ago I took claim to a blind lead and will spend the next few weeks extracting new rock."

"A blind lead? But how did you know? Where is it?"

"Down the hole from the World West mine, a ledge sticking out there. The veins are new ones. It's all done, Auntie. The ledge is mine."

"And you're not planning to share it?"

"Why should I? Found it myself."

"But those nice boys, the Reverend and Samuel, are the ones who found it," said Aunt Sturdy, her legs buckling. She felt lightheaded and sweat poured from her forehead. Stewart caught his aunt and yelled at the woman inside to fetch a fan and some water.

Stewart and the cook girl dragged Aunt Sturdy's ample body inside. They hoisted her, with much difficulty, onto the frame of a cot. The girl fanned her employer's face. The woman hastily covered herself with a wool blanket as Aunt Sturdy came to.

"Lord, haven't I suffered enough, saving countless lives out here in the middle of nowhere? Don't I deserve some riches? Just a little?" She smiled at the cook girl, touched her cheek with a bloated hand, and then sighed. "We will be on our way then." The girl extended her hand to Aunt Sturdy. They exited the tent with Stewart following behind. He heaved Aunt Sturdy and her cook girl into the carriage.

"Before we go, I wonder, how did you find the blind lead?" Aunt Sturdy asked.

"Oh, I knew about it for a long time but had to explore it thoroughly before making my claim." The cook girl looked down at her hands. She clutched the reins tightly and held her breath. She did not dare to look at the man whom she would marry once the silver began to sell. She did not see him wink at her as the horse pulled the two women away.

"What a coincidence," Aunt Sturdy said. "Let's get back and get some rest. We've got to open for breakfast in a few hours time. It's been a long night."

The border collie greeted the women at the back door. "You feed the damn dog," Aunt Sturdy said to the girl. The cook girl did as she was told.

It would be the last time.

Doc Gooding

In this dry lifeless wasteland, he couldn't help but meditate on his more comfortable house in Ocean Park west of Los Angeles and his young, spritely wife and three daughters wearing cotton dresses that matched the fence around his acre of land. His medical practice was thriving as more and more eager Easterners and mid-Westerners arrived and Croatians, Italians, and Irish too, their faces haggard from the travel but their minds quick to seize on opportunities. Doctor Gooding had a practice near Abbot Kinney's ersatz Venice canals and tended to all sorts of odd ailments; he had formed a specialty in foot funguses, viral infections, and malnutrition. He was, to the Water Department's tastes, the perfect man to appoint as Jawbone Division Hospital Steward on the largest engineering project ever attempted in California, the Los Angeles Aqueduct. An endeavor second only to the Panama Canal in scope and ambition, the Aqueduct was a marvelous organism of snaking tunnels, concrete-lined channels, Roman siphons, and that free agent of movement, that force of change and reckoning to which no money was owed, gravity. The City of Los Angeles, with little more than a meek river and decreasing supplies of groundwater, was going to bring water to its citizens from somewhere distant that had plenty to spare, the Owens Valley.

Seven months ago, Doc Gooding had traveled with the chief surgeon in his Franklin car to remote Mojave, where they spent the night at the respectable Harvey House and then departed early the next morning for Cinco by a mule-drawn team hauling freight to the line near the desolate and fiercely windy, blisteringly hot or god-awful cold rough country of Jawbone Canyon. Cinco Hospital suited Doctor Gooding as an outfit with just about all that was required to address wounds, perform surgeries, and maintain and encourage sanitary conditions in the camps. How thousands of men would be able to live so far from home, so far from their wives and children or their sisters or girl-friends, he scarcely could answer. Even more importantly, how would they keep their wits in Jawbone Canyon beneath such a devastating sun? He set to work immediately and consulted *Dryer's Encyclopedia of Ailments, Fungi and Infection in Arid Climates*, a noted British authority. *They ought to know, having been in infernal places like Africa and India for so long*, he thought.

Later in the morning, he kicked the sable dust beneath his leather work boots, paused in front of the latrines, and rubbed his chin. He took out his white kerchief and wiped his brow, adjusted his glasses, which had slid down his slick nose, and shook his head. These flies would not do. They would bring disease and endless nuisance to the men. They were too close to the food. And it was terrible difficult to relieve oneself with the buzzing, winged creatures all about your private parts. *How to engineer a better latrine?* He turned in the direction of the mess house. He would walk until he had the answer. He was a scientist, after all, and the men, well, the boys really, the boys who gave up part of their wages for medical care and health benefits such as the services rendered by Doctor Gooding, would get what they deserved. The boys of nineteen and twenty years of age with their suspenders, crooked felt hats, stained white shirts, worn brown boots. The boys with dreams in their eyes and optimism in their hearts. He reached for his pen and notebook and, not finding them, returned to his quarters.

As he entered his tent, he noticed that his leftover beef steak and peas from the previous night were still on his table. He had drunk too much the night before and forgotten to clean up his dishes. However, no flies gorged on the beef despite evidence of its ripe putrefaction. *Now*, he thought, *how could that be*? With his hands on his hips he examined his abode. The only unique characteristic he observed from other tents was the cool aspect. His tent, he noted, stood in the shadow of a broken down steam shovel. *In the shadow!* He went to his cabinet, poured an ounce of gin, feeling very much like Robert Dryer of the *Encyclopedia of Ailments,* hailed the Queen, and toasted himself. For he had the answer to the problem of the flies. He sought to inform the division engineer and chief clerk.

"Gentlemen, I have discovered how to abate the flies."

"How?" The engineer was now very curious. He had tried to build the latrines so the flies would not touch the food. He had failed and now felt vulnerable and exposed that a doctor was solving his engineering problem.

"Build an entrance to the latrine, a sort of maze that traps the light. Without the light, the flies will not enter." A fly landed on the engineer's arm. He swatted it away.

"Do you figure such a simple solution will work, Doctor?" the engineer asked.

"I beg you to try it. If it does not, I will take personal responsibility."

"Well, we will take your plan under advisement, won't we?" The engineer turned to the chief clerk and, as the doctor retreated, the engineer winked at him.

Doctor Gooding strode with pep as he prepared for his first eye, nose, and throat inspections of the day. He would see as many men as he could in the day and fill out his report for the City by dusk. All that in addition to a bit of scientific discovery. What a day it had already been.

Down the long rows of the men's tents, he heard an excited group talking and laughing. *No doubt one of the Irish told a naughty joke,* he thought. He disregarded the sudden bursts of noise and retired to his tent to prepare for the inspections.

But the noise did not die down. It grew in intensity and eventually the doctor's curiosity compelled him to set aside his protocols. He walked toward the noise some hundred yards off and saw a group of fifty men or more standing near a section of pipe so grand in circumference that a laborer with another on his shoulders could fit inside. They all appeared to be singing, or perhaps reciting poems. Their eyes were focused on a point on top of the pipe, but he could not see what they were looking at. One of the cement mixers spotted him.

"Doctor Gooding! Come over right away!" He was smiling at the doctor, a look of wonder and amusement on his face. The crowd made room for the doctor, pushing him gently forward toward the pipe. Sitting on top, the crisp white folds of her skirt demurely arrayed beneath her, was Mary Parker, a slim but sturdy woman of thirty-three years with high cheekbones, a mass of soft brown hair in an untidy bun, and set of cocky pursed lips.

"What is the matter, Miss?" Doctor Gooding asked the woman. He realized he should have called her Missus but did not see her wedding ring in time.

"Mrs. Parker," she said. Doc removed his hat and leaned forward in a courteous bow. She smiled, and the doctor saw a delicate mole above the corner of her lips. It gave her an allure the doctor quickly tried to dismiss.

"Doctor Lyle Gooding," he replied. He waited for her answer but she gave none. She smiled down on him, a sort of guardian angel, waving her hand at the growing assemblage of men.

Doctor Gooding cleared his throat.

"Mrs. Parker, may I ask what is wrong?"

"Ain't nothing wrong, Doc," a short grizzled man with missing teeth said finally.

"Well, what is this commotion then?" the doctor asked.

"This lady is stoppin' the work today, Doc," the man said, smiling broadly and patting the doctor on the back. "This piece of pipe here is going up Water Canyon to Son-of-a-Bitch Canyon. Beg your pardon, dear lady, but that is its proper name for it is a son-of-a-bitch to us. Back to what I was saying. This lady, she don't want this pipe to go, and so, since it can't go, I can't go and that is why the work is stopping."

"But I don't understand."

"Doctor, I am protesting the work these men are being asked to do," Mrs. Parker said.

"But why?" was all Doc could muster.

"These men are taking our water, Doctor Gooding." She laughed.

"I'm sorry, Mrs. Parker, but how are these honest men taking your water?"

"From what I can tell, the City has squashed the Bureau of Reclamation deal, is going to build a pipeline from the Owens River to your fair city, and will leave our land to dry up, taking our livelihoods in the process. I sit up here in protest."

"Mrs. Parker, you must come down. What you're doing is illegal and I don't want to have to—"

"Call the sheriff?" she said. "I just adore Sheriff Giles and would love to see him." Clearly the law would not persuade her to leave her post.

"We're not taking all of this water, you know," the doctor stammered.

"Oh?"

"No. In fact, even Teddy Roosevelt himself approved this plan. The voters approved it. It's sound engineering. It's the grandest project since the Romans built their aqueducts."

"Yes, yes, I've certainly heard those tired arguments before," Mrs. Parker said. "The greatest good for the greatest number. Yes, those words issued forth from our president. Seems he wants one people to die in sacrifice for another, more important lot of citizens down south. Kill our crops so that San Fernando can have theirs," she said.

"Mrs. Parker, I don't know to what you are referring, but would you please come down before the sheriff, or worse, a City guard, is called."

"Call them all, sir. I beg you," she said, before turning her head to speak to a Bosnian boy named Sanel. The doctor was sure that her rare beauty and disdain for authority were appealing distractions for the female-deprived among the men. He knew he had to put a stop to it all as quickly as possible. But how?

Just then, the engineer and chief clerk pushed through the men, angry that the work had been stopped for nearly an hour. Before the doctor could explain his assessment of the situation to the two men, the division engineer barked an order.

"Doctor, remove this sick woman. She is obviously delirious from the sun exposure and needs to be treated immediately." Both Mrs. Parker and the doctor looked dumbly at the engineer.

"You heard me. Remove her to the hospital at once. Sanel, O'Reilly, hop to it!" The two men shyly lifted Mrs. Parker, who looked neither astonished nor surprised, so that her arms were about their shoulders and her legs were held aloft by their hands, their fingers delicately touching her thighs through the crisp cotton starched that morning. They walked through the swelling crowd and marched away with the doctor in tow.

The small party repaired to the front room of the hospital. The woman's half-smile, half-smirk remained. She did not speak, only watching with gentle authority over the men assembled around her. The division engineer fancied that a proper whipping would put the woman in her place, and that calling her husband, Roy Parker, would fix her up good and put to bed these so-called views.

"Mrs. Parker, you got a lot of nerve disrupting my project here today. If I had half a mind, I'd of hauled you off in the car to the sheriff's office directly, but I'm giving you another chance. Women like you forget your role. You have ideas about yourselves that aren't fitting. It's disgusting." The engineer turned away from the group, shaking his head and pulling a flimsy handkerchief from his pocket to attend to a congested nose. A loud honking blow issued forth from the engineer and Sanel and O'Reilly jumped. The boys were glad to be in the cool room, away from their fellows on the line. They hoped that, if they kept quiet, the engineer wouldn't notice their presence and order them back outside.

"What I'm about to say I don't want to say in polite company," the engineer said. He looked up. "Sanel, O'Reilly, get out," he ordered. The two boys moped out of the tent, looking back at Mrs. Parker, who was sitting up and beaming at their young faces.

"But I don't consider this company all too polite, the doctor excepted," he said, staring right at Mrs. Parker, who did not allow him to penetrate her calm.

"You, woman, are the bile of the Earth, the scourge of our society. You got no right to do what you're doing. You are neglecting your responsibilities, which, from what I've learned, are more than other women since you've got an imbecile son that isn't improvable. You got a husband that has no courage to stay with you. He's so ashamed of your ways and your evil intentions that he left for the hills to go mining. And even in his shame, Mr. Parker's still sending you money, though if it was me, I'd say you don't deserve it. Get out of my camp. Don't you come back again. You don't deserve what this aqueduct will do for you. It's going to make that Owens Valley a place of importance. Right now, it's a failure. A bunch of backward farmers and miners trying to make their money quick and it ain't working. Get out, and if I see you again, it isn't going to be words I'll abuse you with." The engineer raised his fist and grinned, his face a mix of hate and lust, his eyes resting on Mrs. Parker's breasts. He moistened his lips with his tongue, put his hand on the doctor's shoulder, and said, "Drive her back home. And hurry back." Under his breath the engineer said, "Don't want this woman holding us back no more." He stepped out into the searing sun. Then he hesitated, turned and walked back inside, spat on the floor in front of Mrs. Parker, took a final look at her chest, and stomped out.

The doctor, embarrassed by this outburst, stood before Mrs. Parker, stunned. After several moments, he said, "I guess, Mrs. Parker, I can take you back home if you're ready." She had not said anything since being carried down from the pipe and had not nodded or changed the expression on her face.

"Thank you, Doctor, but I will ride my horse home. Sanel tied him in the shade of a steam shovel and was kind enough to bring my horse water."

"I would like to drive you, to get you there faster." What he wanted to say was *I would like to protect you*.

"No thank you, Doctor." She hopped off the examining table, dusted her skirt, and disappeared. The doctor was as confused by her refusal as he was by the scene that had just taken place. He stood erect, unsure of what to do with his day now that it had been interrupted. But he found himself oddly electrified by the whole event, his fingertips tingling and his heart beating as though he had run a race. He quickly turned to his duties, however, when he remembered that his inspections started in twenty minutes, right after the men's lunch. He hastened back to his tent to gather his hardbound ledger and pen. *I should have driven her home.*

After the doctor had seen fifty or so men with their running noses, earaches, and complaints of dry throats and coughs, he sat at his worktable, unable to focus on the report. He glanced through the doorway at the dead sky. He looked at his pocket watch, holding it in his hand and rubbing its brass cover for several minutes, lost in thought. *What's bothering me,* he wondered. He popped open the watch and saw that he had only thirty minutes before the clerk would arrive in his Stoddard-Dayton car to pick up the report. He got to work.

Though the vittles offered hardly satisfied, hunger overcame the men's tastes and they dashed to the mess house. Doctor Gooding took his meal alone in his tent, silent as he speared the limp, stringy meat with his fork.

That night, he did not feel like talking, smoking outside, or playing cards, activities that normally occupied him until late in the evening. He walked until the twilight sky muffled all noise. Then, though quite a distance from camp, he walked even further. The heat had gone, replaced by cooler air that hovered around his head like a mother's hands draped over her children's hair and ears. Soon, he heard nothing but the distant coyotes and scurrying kangaroo rats in the brush. He thought he saw a bat but was unsure. The lights of the stars easily numbered in the thousands, and as he looked toward the outline of the volcanic hills, he thought he saw a raptor soaring above a pile of boulders. He felt comforted by the large winged bird, stately and graceful in its arching flight, soaring effortlessly in the early night sky.

He no longer remembered what had driven him out on this quiet perambulation and turned quickly, suddenly conscious of his sullen and reflective state. He did not like to dwell too long inside his mind. So he shook his head as if to empty it of some murk that had amassed inside and made his way back to camp. But he still did not desire any company so he returned to his tent and to a glass tumbler he filled with whiskey to calm his nerves and help him fall asleep. *Tomorrow I will return to myself,* he thought.

The sun had not yet risen, and Doctor Gooding stared up at the frame of his tent. No one expected him for hours. He went back to bed. A mule train woke him before breakfast, the muleskinners calling out to the animals as sharp snakeskin whips sizzled across the air. In this enterprise to move water, new technologies like steam shovels toiled alongside mules, vestiges of the silver boom. These beasts of patience and endurance, doubled in strings of twenty-four, pulled weighty cargo, their lead bells swinging about their necks.

After lunch, he ordered supplies for the coming month: iodine, cadmium, alcohol, cotton balls, bandages, tape, disinfectant, two iron cots, a stretcher, ipecac syrup, and aspirin. He was methodical, practical, filling out the order slip in a flowing cursive, elegant and exact. Small beads of sweat flowed down his face, his eyeglasses unable to grip his nose.

"Sir, Doctor, there's been an accident." Sanel butted his head in through the hospital office door, and Doc Gooding saw that his eyes were wide with shock, or some strange form of stupefied admiration.

"There's been a terrible spill," he said, and with that vague description, Sanel grabbed the doctor by the upper arm and pulled him out, his pen still in his hand. They ran to the work line. Doctor Gooding thought about what might have spilled and who might be injured, how many people might warrant attention.

What he found was a heap of white muslin skirts and a face obscured by flowing hair, unfastened, he thought, by the fall. It was Mrs. Parker, thrown from her horse, her upper arm bone out of its socket and her lower arm jutting out at an impossible angle from her elbow. He squatted next to her and delicately lifted her wrist, which felt shattered like a cheap china dinner plate, fragmented and loose beneath her skin.

"Sanel, why didn't you tell me it was a fall from a horse?" He inwardly cursed the Bosnian's lack of English and ordered two men to run back to the hospital to fetch a stretcher.

Mrs. Parker rolled her head toward Doctor Gooding and seemed for a moment to be about to say something, but her lips parted only briefly and then returned to a bemused countenance.

"How did this happen?" Doc asked the assembled onlookers. Mrs. Parker answered instead.

"I was riding Candy, my horse here, and she must have seen a rat or a rabbit and it startled her. She set off and reared up so high I nearly slid off. But I held on, which probably made it worse, and she shook like a quaking aspen until I was thrown off. I landed right on the elbow." Mrs. Parker seemed at ease among them and let them look at her outstretched body and the tussled fabric of her shirt. Doc Gooding found himself watching her, disapproving of his own feeling of vulnerability. She was too talkative for an injured, he thought. She must be going into a sort of delirium. He placed his finger over her mouth and whispered, "That's all right, Missus. Just lie there and we'll take care of that arm. It's just pointing in the wrong direction is all. There, there."

Mrs. Parker closed her eyes, and though he tried not to watch her face too closely for fear the men would see, he thought he saw a thin smile appear on her face and a quiet trust in his abilities. It strengthened him as he directed the Bosnian and the Irishman to lift her carefully as he tied the cotton bands delicately across her legs and chest. They kept the stretcher level and steady between them until they reached the hospital.

"I know this will hurt, what you have to do," she said to Doc Gooding when Sanel and O'Reilly placed her on the table.

"I'll give you a little something. It will go down warm and take the worst edge off it," he told her. He poured her two ounces of whiskey and then administered opium pills.

"You'll still feel it, but it won't be nearly as bad," he said. "Just a little sedative." He waited a few minutes before replacing her dislocated shoulder in the socket. She screamed. Then he manipulated the broken pieces of her arm back into place. She nearly passed out. He feverishly tended to her wrist, wrapping it in wet plaster. He fashioned a sling for stability and then fanned Mrs. Parker's skin, which had reddened while he worked. Small drops of sweat dotted her forehead and nose and she rolled her head from side to side. He sponged her face and soothed her as best he could.

When he completed his ministrations, he posted the Bosnian outside of the building. "Don't let anyone in. I don't care if they're on a spree and need tomatoes in a can. I'm curing a real injury here. Keep the drunks out," he told Sanel.

A moment later, the chief engineer strode through the front door before Sanel could give warning to Doc Gooding. After three drinks in the mess house, the chief engineer's unshaven face bristled in alcohol and his sweat-stained shirt clung to his pronounced, distended belly. He chewed on a cigar, its brown paper unraveling inside his gums.

"What's this all about, Doc? We can't have that woman here in the camp." Doc Gooding rose, coolly walking toward the entryway, grasping the thin arm of his eyeglasses and assuming his logical authority in this medical situation.

"Sir, I'm afraid we have no choice. This woman, *Mrs. Parker*," he said with emphasis, "fell on City property. Were we not to see to her, I would be in violation of my oath and the City would be liable for her treatment plus damages." The division engineer removed the cigar, spat on the floor to rid himself of tobacco and paper chunks, and said, "Well, I don't like it. That woman is bad news, Doc, and I want her out of here." He threw down his cigar, failing even to put it out, and turned hastily, barreling through the door. Doc bent down, put his thumb and forefinger around the stub of the cigar, and walked outside to extinguish it. He shook his head.

"Sanel, make sure no one else comes in, won't you?"

"I tried to stop him, sir, but I don't have no authority."

"I know Sanel. It's alright. We need to keep the hospital quiet for Mrs. Parker." He touched Sanel's shoulder and gave a small nod to the youth, who he knew was on his side, the side of healing this woman, no matter her law-breaking ways.

Mrs. Parker's breathing made little in the way of sound. She was still as desert rocks but some color was returning to her face. He watched the flicker of the kerosene lamp on her cheeks. The air was still soothing and warm, and for a few moments, he did not lift his gaze from her face.

"You will have to come back for check-ups and for your medicine," he said softly. He turned to his thick ledger on the side table and searched for a piece of lead. Once he found one, he wrote a prescriptive care recommendation in his quick scrawl. He tore out the paper and placed it underneath an orange-red volcanic rock.

"I will need to see you every day this week," he said aloud. It would be a rigorous program of rehabilitation, but her arm had broken at the elbow and her wrist called for daily attention to rebuild what had shattered. "Yes, you will need a number of visits." Suddenly, he realized how tired he was, how he held so much worry, taut and inflexible, in the small of his back. He yawned and removed his glasses. He took the bed closest to Mrs. Parker and reclined for a brief nap. He awoke what seemed like hours later, but by the increasing din of the men's poker games down the line of tents, it could only have been half an hour, he guessed. He could hear Mrs. Parker speaking and realized he had turned over on his side away from her. She was repeating something.

"But it's so far."

He pushed himself upright. "What is so far, Mrs. Parker?"

"It's so far. To come. I cannot come every day."

"Mrs. Parker, I'm not sure I take your meaning."

"Doctor, I cannot come for treatments."

"Oh?"

"It's my husband."

"Well, you didn't seem to take that into consideration when you started protesting, Mrs. Parker." She looked down and cried.

"I'm sorry, I spoke rashly. Please, tell me why you cannot come."

"I cannot come."

"We'll need to rehabilitate that arm. I hope you know just how badly injured you are."

"Yes, I know."

"Then stop this nonsensical talk. You'll come if I have to pick you up in the Franklin," he said with more force than he meant.

"He will prevent that."

"What do you mean?"

"I have to take care of William, my son. He has a touch of something not very common around here."

"I know about your son's feeblemindedness. I'm afraid medicine is not yet certain about treating children like him. However, Mrs. Parker, I can help you. There are institutions for boys and girls where they are better suited to live, beautiful places like farms. But if you don't come, your arm won't heal and you could be in continual pain the rest of your life. Then you won't be able to help your son. I'm sorry, Mrs. Parker, but my oath prevents me from permitting that to happen."

"Roy doesn't know I'm here. I left William with Birdie Batch. She has a way with him. He's calmer near her than with me. Sometimes I can't manage him at all. Roy says it's my fault he's such a bad boy."

"Mrs. Parker, you will come see me?"

A cooling wind began blowing through the screen door. The only things he heard were brush rats and birds.

"Oh, I expect you will, I have no doubt of that. You'll come and all the men on the line will salute you and take their hats off to you." He coughed, startled by his brashness, his forward comment revealing too much. *She has made a mark on me.*

"Well then, if I get going now, I'll be home in time to make breakfast tomorrow and pick up William and take him to church. I might have some spare moments to set down some words, too," she said.

"Words?"

"I'm writing about the land, the miners, your men, the Indians, the irrigation ditches, the morning light off the Inyo Mountains, cloud-bursts, just what I see. I know you're going to say a lady hasn't a right or a talent to do man's writing. Well, I tell you, I do it and probably better than many men."

"I wouldn't dare say that a lady couldn't write as well as a man, if not better. I just wonder how you'll be writing. These injuries will prevent you from working. You'll need to do a full program of rehabilitative exercises. It is all here in my prescription. Some are painful and will require your full attention. You could bring William here. It might do him well to be outdoors. You're going to have to tell your husband, you know."

"Please stay out of my affairs. I will do as I please. I always have. I'm riding home. I'll be just fine."

"You're not riding back to your house."

"How else would I get home?"

"Not on that horse. I don't want you to be thrown again."

"Nonsense! Most reliable horse I ever had. Just a little spooked, that's all. Happens to every horse."

"Mrs. Parker, you're being unreasonable. You cannot ride your horse and you cannot go home right now. You still have opium in your system. You are no doubt still drowsy and incapable of handling your horse. I won't hear of it."

"Well then, chase me in your fancy contraption, that Franklin car you bring from the City. I'm leaving. I have duties to attend to and can't afford to waste more time here tonight. Thank you for your services and I hope you and your City managers realize what damage you are about to do."

"Mrs. Parker, the City means you no harm."

"But you'll harm me anyway. You'll hurt the land, too. Please, Doctor, let me be."

Mrs. Parker feebly rocked upward, hoping the motion would lift her off the bed. She tried several times to rise but each time fell backward in a heap. At last, she made it up. The blood had flooded her head and she felt queasy, began sweating uncontrollably, made as if to vomit, and then fainted. Doc Gooding's arms reached her back and shoulders in time and she fell neatly into his sturdy frame. He laid her back on the bed, straightened her legs, being careful not to touch her skin, and pulled the blanket over her hips.

"Have it your way," he said gently. After several minutes, she opened her eyes and looked searchingly into his face.

"I am your prisoner, dear Doctor. Won't you send word to my neighbor, Miss Birdie?" Doc Gooding nodded, wiped a strand of hair from her forehead, and paused. He fluffed the pillows behind her back and turned the lamp low enough so that she closed her eyes and fell quickly to sleep.

Doc Gooding kept a close eye on her throughout the night, sleeping but an hour himself. He rose an hour before dawn, just as the moon descended beyond the borders of the Sierra, and made himself coffee back in his tent, changing his underclothes and shaving the stubble that had grown overnight. Just then, an automobile pulled up outside the hospital.

Doc hurried to meet the car, his face towel still in his hands. The driver, all mustache, goggles, and wool driving cap with leather bill, emerged from a Stoddard-Dayton car. Doc noticed the driver's generously scuffed knee-high boots with the pant legs tucked inside. Across the driver's healthy chest a well-used pair of powerful binoculars on a strap seemed at the ready. It was the chief of the City's water department, in the flesh, unaccompanied, out of the blue.

The chief did not greet Doc Gooding as he breezed into the hospital and stopped in front of Mrs. Parker. Doc Gooding walked in behind him, perplexed but offering pleasantries nonetheless. "Good morning, sir, how was your trip? Would you like some coffee? I've just made a pot. I hope the camp meets with your approval and that the reports have been satisfactory. The incidences of disease and fungus are extremely low here, sir. Sir?"

The chief pulled up a chair, cleared his throat, and barked, "Missus! Missus, wake up now! I've got to talk to you. Doctor, you'll leave us alone so we can speak privately please." Doc Gooding backed up, knocking over a stand containing a bottle of iodine, the contents of which spilled out as the bottle broke in two. He nervously picked up the shards and looked for a moment at Mrs. Parker, who smiled at him as he walked outside.

When the chief came out ten minutes later, he finally acknowledged the doctor.

"Terrific job here, young man. Your hospital is first rate, and I've been pleased by the progress made here. And that woman." Here, he stopped and leaned toward the much taller Doc Gooding, who could smell onions and coffee on the chief's breath. "That woman understands what's happening here better than anyone else. Take care of her, see to it that she receives good and complete care, but then we must prevent her from coming back. Understand?"

"Of course, sir."

"Oh, another thing, Doctor. Stick with medicine. Leave latrines and flies to the engineers." The chief replaced his driving cap atop his head of plentiful white hair and did an about-face.

During his small lunch of peas and mashed potatoes—the heat had ruined the rest of the meat—Doc Gooding reached for the bundle of parcels the chief had brought for him. A letter from his father, one from his sister in Missouri, a crate full of tomatoes for curing the drunks, ten bottles each of castor oil, iodine, and alcohol. Also, two letters from his wife. He reached for his bottle of whiskey and poured a generous glass for himself.

He could not recall this feeling of tender excitement and anticipation, not even when he courted his wife. He opened one of her letters but placed it on the bed unread. He sat staring at the washbasin, uncertain what had come over him. Why did he feel a burning for Mrs. Parker? Why did he scarcely consider his three children?

This new sensation radiated, a delicate flutter across his chest and down to his groin, a physical response he was marveled and ashamed by at the same time. He wanted to be with his patient. He wanted to touch her and look upon her. He knew it was treacherous, but he rose, drank the remainder of his whiskey, and strode back to the bed where she lay.

He walked to her side. She was slurping hot soup prepared by the cook, and he knelt, took the bowl from her, wrapped his hands about her small warm fingers, and lowered his mouth to meet them.

"You've been drinking, Doctor."

He smiled, leaned closer, and kissed her forehead, inhaled her scent of sage and lemon oil, soap and desert air. She relaxed into his attentions and put her good arm around his head, pulling his hair gently in small strokes down his neck and back. They looked at one another. The good doctor rose from his knees, pulled a screen about the bed, and lay himself beside her, careful not to touch her damaged arm. He kissed her mouth, eyelids, ears, neck, and breastbone. He had never touched any other with such relish and abandon.

"Men cheapen this with visits to the whore house. I hope that's not what this is to you," she said. He squeezed her frame close and spoke soft, "No, no, not to me."

"I've never been cherished," she said. He licked her tears and touched his forehead to hers. They stayed that way for long, lingering minutes, the length of his torso touching every part of hers.

Aqueduct workers returning from a weekend at the Mojave saloons began arriving in camp, sickly and weak, their drunken binges having exhausted their paychecks and their already thin bodies desperate for nutrition and water. Doc Gooding did not want to leave his patient, but the day was waning and the week about to begin.

When Doc's whiskey had worn off, he rose to splash water on his face. Mrs. Mary Parker was able to stand. She asked Sanel the Bosnian to drive her home. Before she descended the hospital's front steps, she turned. He wanted to say something to her but just returned her regard, like a man before a gallows.

That night, four beds were taken with sick men. Some had vomited multiple times and were dry heaving, their delicate stomach linings defeated by the whiskey they had consumed. Doc Gooding busied himself with their care, trying not to think about his betrayal. At midnight, the four men were asleep and had appeared to stabilize with the concoction Doc had created to dry the men out and restore their appetite—stewed tomatoes served directly from the can plus castor oil, salt, and camphor, followed by lead and opium pills.

Doc returned to his tent, imagining Mrs. Parker watching him as he kicked some pumice stone down the lane. Though no one stirred, he was in her company. He pictured her following behind, noting his gait, observing his hands as they traveled from his pockets to his hair and then to his rumpled wool shirt, which he straightened. He could smell her damp hair and see her speckled grey-blue eyes. He knew what he had to do. Doc Gooding found the engineer's car, rolled it out to the road, and drove it to the Harvey House in Mojave, where the quiet streets seemed to need stillness to recover from the weekend tear. It was half past one in the morning.

He thought of going inside to request a room but decided against it. He parked facing the train tracks, silver-lined under the moon. Doc pulled an envelope and a piece of stationery from his chest pocket, unfolded the paper, and began to write.

Dear Division Chief, he wrote, *I tender this resignation from my post as Cinco Hospital Steward, Jawbone Division, effective immediately.*

He signed the letter and inserted it into the envelope. He walked to the lobby and slipped the letter under the door where the stationmaster would see it in the morning. He crumpled down onto a bench, his head in his hands, trying to conjure the petite frame of his wife and his three growing children, the neat fence around the Ocean Park cottage, just whitewashed last spring, and the yellow azaleas and very feminine pink camellias growing so easily in the sun. He saw the sign hung out front, hand-painted: *Doctor Lyle Gooding, Family Doctor.*

Appearing out of the shadows, a solitary black bear mounted the platform. The bear, a mere ten steps from Doc, knocked over a rubbish bin and began sifting through the contents. Doc Gooding sat frozen, unsure of what to do. While he watched the bear, a cloud covered the moon and a wind whipped from behind, chilling him. He realized he had forgotten his coat. The bear, engrossed in its treasure of food scraps, took no notice of Doc Gooding. Eventually, the bear descended the train platform. The moon traveled across the sky and was replaced by the wash of sunrise. Lead bells pierced the silence as unencumbered mule trains sprinted toward the station. Doc made for the car, pulling away before anyone should see him.

He drove north toward where he knew Mrs. Parker lived.

The Walker Boys
and the Alabama Gates

Against the Alabama Hills, named for a Confederate ship sunk thousands of miles away from the Owens Valley, perched a simple white guardhouse above a control gate capable of rebellion every day, which is probably why it was also named after that Confederate boat. The contraption was called the Alabama Gates and its three chutes led from the guardhouse down a steep incline to a spillway below that was almost always empty, as it was used only in case of emergency floods. Normal operation meant the steel door gates were lowered and locked into place to permit unimpeded flow of the City's water down the artificial river, a concrete-lined cradle rocking its baby all the way to Los Angeles. Inside the guardhouse, the City's watchman, Leonard Bent, finished what little work there was each day by noon. With so many hours to fill, whiskey and solitaire had become the watchman's constant companions.

Below, El Camino Sierra simmered in the heart-crushing heat, motorists stopping frequently to add water to their radiators from dull-colored canisters.

Leonard Bent failed to notice young Harvey Walker entering the Alabama Gates guardhouse one summer afternoon in 1925, absorbed as he was in the Dodge Brothers Coach that two other Walker brothers used as a distraction during what could best be described as a theft. Harvey's older brother, Mickey, and younger brother, Benjamin, like salesmen slick and assured, waxed about the Coach's new features, their arms draped around Leonard like a beloved uncle. "Here," they said, "squeeze right on in there, sit behind the steering wheel, see how it feels." Leonard admitted he would be much obliged to do just that so Mickey and Benjamin squished Leonard inside the Coach. All the while, Harvey Walker was above, inside the guardhouse, buttoning his wool shirt over the gate operation manual he had just found in Leonard's desk. Harvey rejoined the men at the Coach and bid Leonard a good afternoon and then drove his brothers to Mount Whitney Fish Hatchery to draw their battle plan.

The Walker brothers leaned and worried over the manual, so engrossed that they did not hear Marty McDougal's Ford or his footsteps.

"Well, if it isn't the sons of the Walker Cattle Ranch. What you gentlemen got there?" Marty McDougal approached the picnic table beneath the cottonwoods. The younger boys were quiet. Mickey Walker, the oldest at nineteen, answered. "Hello there, Mr. McDougal," he said.

"We're just planning a drive. Thought we might pull over here at this lovely hatchery for a drink of water. Awful hot today." He fanned his reddened face with his hat. Harvey, whose face bore fresh evidence of his lack of dexterity when it came to shaving, hastily stuffed the manual into his back pocket. Benjamin, the youngest and just-turned-teenager, removed his hat and wiped his forehead against his sleeve, looking at the ground.

"I'm mighty proud of this hatchery, boys. The Tudor tower, the long white shiny room full of tubs brimming with growing fish, the lush grass lawns, the pond full of trout. Isn't it a sight? I hear there's even going to be a wedding here next week, the bride thought it so suitable."

Marty McDougal presented himself as an adopted son and savior of the Owens Valley. His gratitude to the citizens was manifested in this hatchery, a veritable temple to the Golden Trout. He would turn the empty mountain streams and the Owens River into waters of gold to save them all.

The fishermen were arriving thanks to Marty's brochures opining the most beautiful fish in the world, the elusive, unique, mystical fish from heaven, the Golden Trout. Its olive-green skin, bold spots, bright red lateral stripe, and golden red belly were the colors of dreams. A day spent in an alpine stream, knee high in glacial waters, capped by the catching of a Golden Trout, was a day to be remembered.

"Well, where's your road map you got there taking you boys today?" Marty McDougal looked straight at Harvey Walker, who shot a questioning glance at Benjamin Walker, who turned to the older brother, Mickey. "Sorry, we must be on our way. Have to pick up Mother; she needs to see a doctor," Mickey said.

"I thought you said you were out for a drive," Marty McDougal said.

"Oh, we were, but Mother has an appointment. She's been ill," Mickey said as he and his brothers hopped into their Dodge.

"Well, I hate to run. Nice seeing you, Mr. McDougal," Mickey said. Funny, Marty McDougal thought, Mrs. Walker always seemed so robust and healthy. Perhaps he would go to Lone Pine and pay her a visit tomorrow.

"Hope she is feeling better then. Give her my best," Marty McDougal shouted at the car. He wiped his brow with his handkerchief.

The three boys drove down Whitney Fish Hatchery Road to the El Camino Sierra, turning right to drive south to the Alabama Gates.

"Now that we have the plans for the Alabama Gates, we have to do something," Mickey said.

"Blackmail Leonard Bent!" Harvey suggested.

"He don't care if we have possession of the plans," Mickey said. "What I'm thinking is publicity against the City."

"You mean how they begun installing those turbine wells to pump more from the ground?" Harvey asked.

"That and with this drought we're in, the aqueduct's not giving the City enough water. They want more," Mickey said.

"I hear the City's going to put in more than fifty of those

wells all around the northern part of the Owens River. Not only are they taking the water on top of the land, but now they're taking the water below it." Benjamin Walker spit on the ground and crossed his arms. "Pa's fields are already drying up."

"City's happy to have everything go back to its desert-like ways," Mickey said. "Well, what are we going to do?" asked Harvey.

"We'll take it all back. We'll open the emergency spillway at the Alabama Gates," Mickey said. "Whoever controls the gate commands the aqueduct."

"We'll be arrested," Benjamin said.

"That's right. And we'll be in the *Register*, the *Herald*, and the *Daily Times*. We need to get attention boys," Mickey said. He continued, "We'll plan to distract Leonard Bent again. Harvey, can you sneak out some of Pa's whiskey? And a package of cigars from Mr. Dell's storeroom?"

"You know me, clever as a City engineer," said Harvey.

Later that afternoon, Leonard Bent played solitaire while Marty McDougal drove back to Independence for a meeting with a movie director.

As Marty McDougal approached the courthouse in Independence, he decided to see about Mrs. Walker. She was one of the nicest women in the valley and he felt obliged to check in on her and see if there was anything he could do. *I should have offered my help to the boys*, Marty McDougal chided himself. He left word with Mr. Dell, the grocer, that he would meet the movie director for dinner instead. He pushed the car as fast as it would go and headed south to Lone Pine, passing a pear orchard with half-dead trees.

Back at the Alabama spillway, the boys pulled up on the short dirt road to the guardhouse. Leonard Bent rose when he saw the familiar car. He opened the door and waved. He was glad to see the Walker brothers again. They were good boys, he thought. Always went to church with their mother, did as they was told. They would take over the Walker Cattle Ranch someday and that was a thing to be proud of.

"Mr. Bent, I'm just out for a drive with my brothers here. Father wanted me to give you something," said Mickey.

"Come in boys. I got the fan blowing and if you hold a wet cloth to your faces you might feel a bit of relief." Mickey placed a brown bag on a sturdy wooden table against the cleanly washed window inside the guard's room.

"What's that you boys got?" Leonard asked.

"A gift from my Pa," Mickey said. "I didn't look at what it was. Pa said he owed you for the sugar Mother borrowed last week." Leonard smiled and unwrapped the brown package.

"Well I'll be. Your father shouldn't have. Oh, and cigars too! He's always been nothing but friendly to me." Leonard seemed lost in a sentimental thought as he held the bottle of tawny liquid. He shook his head. The boys watched him closely.

"What do you boys say? Promise not to tell your mother and I'll give each of you a sip and a puff." The three boys smiled.

"Oh no, Mr. Bent, we don't want to disturb you," said Benjamin.

"We wouldn't want to get you in trouble with the department neither," said Mickey.

"Hell boys, no one sees me here. Only got to file a report once a month and even then no one reads it anyhow. Come on, let's have a little sip. Just one?"

"Well, okay, but only if you show us how you play solitaire," Benjamin said. Leonard Bent rubbed his hands together.

"Go ahead and time me if you like. I'm the best, fastest solitaire player in the Owens Valley." Leonard Bent crossed the small room, opened a wooden hutch, and reached for two glasses and a box of matches.

"We'll have to share our glasses, boys. Not used to having company here." Leonard poured a generous portion of whiskey in each glass and lit four cigars.

"Now don't drink it fast. Do that and you'll be dizzier than a drunk Indian. Little sips boys. Now for the real show." Leonard sat at the table, his teeth clenching his cigar, and motioned for the boys to do the same. He shuffled his red Bicycle deck of cards so fast that the whizzing punctuated the still air.

Leonard Bent proceeded to deal himself a game of solitaire. And another. And a third, a fourth, and a fifth. He drank the moonshine between games. So far, his record was three and a half minutes. By the sixth game, Harvey, who had only pretended to drink the potent whiskey, said he needed to go for a piss. He excused himself and snuck around the guard station to the spillway gates.

The current of the water in the aqueduct below was imperceptible. Harvey gazed down the channel and thought about how this water, so carefully contained, would flow so far away and that a boy, maybe one his own age, would take a drink or help his own Pa water an orchard of oranges near Los Angeles, all with Owens River water.

He could hear Mickey, Benjamin, and Leonard laughing inside the guardhouse. He didn't have much time. He took a deep breath, walked to the control wheel, and began to turn the hot, thick steel.

It yielded none too easily. But he turned it with all of his will until the gears unlocked. Harvey counted to three, grounded his feet, bent his knees, and used all his weight to push against the lever that would lift the three gates simultaneously. His shoulder pressed on the lever and sweat poured down his temples. He could hear the low wail of the metal gears awakening as the gates rose. A suction sound followed, and the water leaped through the gates and sailed effortlessly back to the dry bed of the Owens River.

When Harvey returned to the guardhouse, Leonard Bent was holding his sides, laughing and snorting. The brothers slapped one another on the back and head, giggling. The boys seemed to have forgotten why they had come. They didn't notice the smile of victory on Harvey's face nor the sound of thundering water.

Marty McDougal grew more worried as he drove. He hoped that Mrs. Walker hadn't caught the measles that Mr. Dell's wife had last month. Mrs. Walker was a strong supporter of Marty's, and he couldn't afford to lose her enthusiasm for the Valley Improvement Projects and his tourism schemes.

He was a quarter mile from the Alabama Gates when he saw the spray from the cascading water. There was a sound like a train barreling down the line. There, he saw an emergency that would require immediate action. Mrs. Walker could wait. The spillway gates were open and a torrent of water was flowing down the channel back to the Owens River.

It was impressive. The water, so placid in the aqueduct, was now a roaring beast. It leaped toward the desert floor and the wide, empty gully where the river used to be.

Marty McDougal's eyes followed the channel up the hill to the gatehouse. There, he saw a slight figure in shadow unfurling an American flag and attaching it to the electricity pole adjacent to the gatehouse. Marty McDougal turned off the El Camino Sierra, parked below the guardhouse, and turned off the engine. He opened the car door and dashed up to a stinking outhouse, where he could not be seen. But Marty McDougal had a view into the guardhouse where he saw two Walker brothers drinking and patting Leonard Bent on the back. All were laughing and waving their hands wildly. Mrs. Walker would be none too pleased to see her good boys partaking in the devil's own drink.

Marty McDougal was unsure what to do. Two boys were drunk and one of them was hoisting the Stars and Stripes aloft as water was going to waste below. He watched as a

Walker brother placed a control wheel into a flour sack and darted back to the Dodge Brothers Coach.

A breeze began to blow as a cloud suddenly appeared to cover the bright sun. Marty McDougal felt a raindrop on his cheek. Impossible, he thought. It never rains this time of year.

Marty McDougal emerged from behind the outhouse, waving his arms. "Walker! You come back here. You stop this nonsense immediately!" But Harvey did not hear. The sound of the water was too loud.

Marty McDougal wiped his cheek. The light wind continued to blow. Harvey Walker returned from the Dodge, grinning with giddy delight. He stopped when he saw Marty McDougal.

"Come here, boy. I said come here!" Marty McDougal's peach skin was red as barn paint. "What is the meaning of this?" he bellowed.

"Mr. McDougal, sir, no offense against you or nothing, but this water is ours. We're just taking it back." Harvey put his hands on his hips and turned to face the river he had recreated.

"This is the only place I can live in and I'm going to stay here until I die from natural causes. They can't make me leave. I'm American. I'm free. We are all free. They can't drive us out of our valley. It's ours," Harvey Walker said.

The door to the gatehouse opened. Leonard Bent emerged, whacking his thighs over some joke. He stumbled toward the footbridge over the aqueduct. Something was wrong, he noticed; the normally still water was escaping at a rapid pace. He felt cool air on his face and wondered why it was suddenly so dark outside. He looked up toward the sun, noticed a bruise-colored cloud covering it, and then saw the American flag waving against the sky. Leonard Bent felt queasy and fell to the ground as he blacked out.

Mickey and Benjamin rushed to Leonard's side. Mickey held Leonard Bent's head in his arms and waved a handkerchief in his face. Harvey turned back to the guardhouse and saw the boys with the fallen Leonard Bent.

Marty McDougal stormed down the hill to crank his Ford and begin driving north to the sheriff's office. As he drove, heavy rain began to fall. Water was everywhere, washing down from the Alabama Gates, bearing down on the road, and draining from the heavens. Blinding sheets, no match for the Ford's wiper blades, saturated Marty McDougal's view of the road. He cursed for the first time in years. The drops slammed against the car and windshield so hard they seemed to be attacking. Ferocious, biting wind now accompanied the precipitation. Though Marty had decelerated the Ford to a crawl, it was still too fast to avoid a newly exposed oil slick. The car careened off the roadway and, in a few short seconds, was lodged in a rut, two wheels spinning in the air, unable to find traction. Marty was stuck. Rain pelted his face, and when he attempted to roll the windows up, he found them stuck too. He reached into the back seat to fetch a blanket he kept on hand and wrapped it around his shoulders while he waited. Surely help would arrive soon.

Hours passed as the storm moved through the valley. Eventually, the sun reappeared. Marty McDougal dozed. At last, a motorist stopped and assisted Marty McDougal with a good shove to move the Ford out of the ditch. It was Tom Mix, the cowboy actor! Marty McDougal pressed his perspiring hands into the star's hands. "Anything I can do for you, Mr. Mix, you just say the word. I am connected to the City, see, and with access to folks that can help publicize your film."

"Oh, my movie's getting upstaged right now. Just back from a takeover at the Alabama Gates. Big picnic up there, the women under Mrs. Glasscock's supervision each made a pie. I played some songs, and butchers from Bishop donated beef for a cookout. A right holiday, you ought to see it. That river is flowing down the chutes like a waterfall!"

The valley had its evil, but it wouldn't sully Marty McDougal's opinion of the majority. The citizens could protest all they liked. The future was already here, whether they wanted it or not. Like the ancient Romans and their aqueducts, Marty McDougal and his City were doing their part to move the water from this empty land to a place more promising, profitable, and agreeable with the masses.

Back at the Alabama Gates, Leonard Bent gnawed on a barbequed drumstick and continued his drunken tear. The Walker brothers drank coffee with the butchers, the pie makers and the citizens who had come to gather around a bonfire to hear them tell and re-tell their tale of deception and thievery.

"We're with you boys," an old rancher, one of the first in the Owens Valley, said. "Here with you as long as it takes. They can't drive us out." Then, as the fire's sparks climbed up into the darkness, a fiddler from Tom Mix's orchestra struck up a reel. Harvey Walker leaped up and sought the hand of a young lady who had been smiling at him across the bonfire. Harvey lifted and turned her around as the fiddle's notes filled the Alabama Hills, her skirts flying until the finish.

Mrs. Hanson

Mrs. Hanson's apple orchard and general store had waited on Round Valley and its farmers for many years, strengthening the fibers of this small frontier with supplies such as coffee, tobacco, overalls, and soap. But for all the bold, sharp-toothed peaks towering above and the well-built men and women who lived below, Round Valley's once flourishing green fields and rows of fruit had faded and shriveled. The newspaper decried an agricultural mecca in decline. Others, chiefly Paiute mothers and fathers and their eagle and coyote spirits, accepted this change from abundance to scarcity—the journey demanded it of them. Burdens once carried by brown people now belonged in equal measure to white people. Mrs. Hanson's neighbors had all sold out to the City in the fall of 1931, save for Mr. Stevens, who was about to. She didn't want to give in.

"God's on their side, not mine," Mrs. Hanson whispered and stepped onto the front porch to shake the dust from a rug. *The City needs more water, and they will get it every time they come for it*, she thought. She hung the rug on the wooden railing and walked around the back of the house, looking up at the chain of mountains. *If only God had given us more snow, the City wouldn't need my land.*

"They can have the fifteen thousand dollars. I don't want money, I want my home," she said aloud. She talked to herself frequently these days. She had also noticed that she often forgot where she was going and had to pause to recall what it was she was about to do. She shook her head as if to rearrange her thoughts and turned back. As she approached the front corner of the house, she noticed a piece of red wood from a child's toy lying behind a dying rose bush. She hadn't noticed it before—the plant had begun to lose its flowers and leaves to dehydration. A stained string clung to the wood—Busby's miniature red wagon, a toy that one of the customers had offered to him on his fifth birthday. Lolly had chased Busby in a jealous rage because she was not given a toy too. Mrs. Hanson smiled and shook her head again. Today was no day for thinking about happier times.

The City didn't want her orchard or her general store. They didn't want the view of Mount Tom or the vista across the valley of pale-pink tablelands created from the eruption of an ancient volcano. The City would abandon her home to the desert rabbit brush and destroy the dirt road that led to her front porch. Bulldozers would ravage the storage barns and the grain silo, one of the first in the valley. Her trees and lawns and the paint on her white fences would weather and turn brown. The life that had existed here would be erased, and all reminders of backbreaking work and toil would become invisible on the horizon.

What the City wanted was simple—her water.

No one could say that Mrs. Hanson hadn't put up a fight. Mr. Thompson from the City had paid her a visit in the spring. Mr. Thompson, a small, elegant man with a thin, graying mustache and wearing a blue suit with an off-white, silk handkerchief tucked carefully into the chest pocket, had been warned about the lonely old woman losing her mind.

"Mrs. Hanson, I am Mr. Thompson, a representative from the City of Los Angeles, and I am interested in buying your property," he said, tipping his hat.

"I know who you are, and I'm not interested, Mr. Thompson," Mrs. Hanson said. "I raised my children here. My husband and I built this orchard up. We constructed all the buildings here—the store, the silo, the barn. I'm very proud of the fences. My son, Busby, whitewashes them every season. And my daughter, Lolly, helps me in the store. Everyone buys from us. What are they all going to do if I sell? Where are they going to get their baking powder, their thread, their machine oil, the ladies their hose? No, I'm surely not interested. You go back to your Big City and you tell them the people here are not about to give up."

Mr. Thompson said, "But Mrs. Hanson, I understand your family is gone. And five of your neighbors are going to sell. You'll be here all alone." Mrs. Hanson had been preparing beef for a church dinner and was holding a butcher knife at her side.

"Mr. Thompson, I told you no. I'm telling you no one more time. If you don't kindly leave my property, I might have to use this knife on your throat instead of on my meat for the church feast."

"What church is that, Mrs. Hanson?"

"Presbyterian, just down the road."

"Mrs. Hanson, that church closed two years ago."

"You're trying to steal my water and my land!"

"I am paying you a fair price, Mrs. Hanson! Giving you more money than you could ever expect to earn by staying."

Mrs. Hanson hoisted the knife above her head and flashed her teeth until Mr. Thompson, dumbstruck, clumsily backed off the porch.

"There isn't enough water for the both of us, Mr. Thompson," she yelled as the frightened man ran down the road to his parked car. "We were here first, it's our water," she screamed.

The water that had irrigated her Winesap apples stopped flowing shortly after Mr. Thompson's visit. All through the valley the City had begun tapping underground waters, leaving irrigation ditches dry, alfalfa crops and apples to rot.

The summer air flowed down from the chalk bluffs across the valley, coming on strong as an oven. Mrs. Hanson recalled her husband's clever solution to the unbearable summer temperatures inside the house. The cottonwoods he had planted behind the house kept the parlor cool in summer. She remembered how proud he was that he could provide comfort to her during her pregnancies. As these fond recollections faded, the apples outside the window came into sharper focus. They were lying in disarray, putrefied on the ground.

Down the road she could see Mr. Stevens, a tall, wiry man with an uneven gait. A log that had fallen on him more than twenty years ago in the forests in Mono County had injured his left leg. Mr. Stevens served as an unofficial veterinarian. He was coming to help with her cat, Worthy.

Mrs. Hanson had acquired Worthy when his mother, a stray with brown and gray stripes, had a litter of kittens some sixteen years ago. The children had begged her to keep a few of the kittens. Mrs. Hanson had refused, saying that they were not responsible enough yet, that she would end up taking care of them. The families adjacent to the orchard adopted the kittens. But one, an orange runt with a nose for field mice and rabbits, kept coming by the back porch. Busby secretly fed the little tabby with white paws some of the chicken from his dinners and the cat returned. Mrs. Hanson finally relented and agreed that a cat might kill some of the mice present in the house.

Since then, Worthy had been her lap cat and constant companion. He slept in the crook of her neck at night and softly breathed into her ear. Mrs. Hanson would never admit it, but the cat had endeared himself to her, relieving her of the loneliness of the property without her husband and children. Busby had died of pneumonia before his fifteenth birthday. Mr. Hanson, sick with the death of his son, died of a broken heart a few months later. And Lolly moved to Palo Alto four years ago to join her professor husband. Before she left, Lolly begged her mother to sell out, abandon the wasteland that was Round Valley, and come with her to be taken care of proper.

Lolly's letter with train tickets to San Francisco had arrived two months ago. Lolly was to install her mother at the progressive and peaceful Agnews State Mental Hospital.

Mr. Stevens had agreed last week to chloroform Mrs. Hanson's cat. She had explained, "I can't take Worthy with me. The insane asylum won't let him in."

"Mrs. Hanson, you're not going to an insane asylum. I've read the papers and seen the pictures of the clock tower and the pretty palms. There are music salons, gardens— shoot, even cows and sheep to remind you of Round Valley! I wish I was going with you, to tell the truth."

"And I can't leave him be to live on rats who have diseases or be killed by the hoodlums down on Line Street. You heard what those Smith boys done to the Woods' cat?"

Mr. Stevens nodded. He had removed the dead tortoiseshell cat himself from the Woods' mailbox. He'd given a stern warning to the Smith twins never to kill another cat unless they would like to be stuffed into a mailbox themselves. Then he forced the Smith twins to clean manure from his ranch for two months.

Mrs. Hanson permitted herself the small luxury of a memory of twenty-two years earlier, when Busby was two years old. Lolly wasn't even born yet. Mrs. Hanson had stood where she was now, feet planted firmly on the wooden planks of the steps, watching as her husband made calculations in his thick red accounting book. It was harvest time and seven young men from Bishop were picking apples as Busby played beneath their ladders. She saw their old sheepdog, Maze, lick Busby's face. Her husband rose from his makeshift desk on their porch and walked past her into the orchard. He picked up Busby, grabbed an apple from one of the baskets, and returned to his wife, who was now mending one of his Sunday shirts. "This is the best one of the day," he said. She smiled and took it from his hands. Indeed, it was the crispest, tastiest apple. Each day Mr. Hanson would bring her the most superior apple for her to try. Fruit grown with one's own hands tasted full of life itself.

The sound from Mr. Stevens' lopsided walk interrupted her reverie. He called out a "hello there" from the gate to her yard. She sighed as her eyes followed the chipped paint of the fence and the dust beyond it.

"Well, Mr. Stevens, did you bring the chloroform?" she asked.

Mr. Stevens had put to sleep many a sick pet rat, rabbit, hamster, and guinea pig for the neighbors. He had perfected the amount of chloroform to soak into gauze or cotton and had built a special airtight container out of metal gas tanks to do it quickly. He didn't like to see an animal, or its human companion, suffer. Children seemed to understand that, when it was time, Mr. Stevens would be there to comfort both the animal and the child.

The tabby was stretched out in the parlor on the back of the couch, sphinxlike, watching a fly that had entered a hole in the screen door. His head jerked up, sideways, and down, following the fly's movements. Mrs. Hanson took a breath, gathered Worthy in her arms, and walked back onto the porch.

"I got him," she said to Mr. Stevens.

He said, "Okay then" and placed the container on a table between two wooden rocking chairs that had defined the Hanson porch for over thirty years. He took a small, rusty flask from his trousers, two pieces of gauze, and a pair of leather gloves. He didn't look up from the table, but he knew Mrs. Hanson was beginning to cry. He put on the gloves. Worthy tried to squirm out of Mrs. Hanson's arms, but she squeezed and cooed softly to him.

"It's going to be all right, Worthy." She sniffed back tears and began to bounce Worthy against her chest as though he were a baby. "I'm going to miss you. I don't know what I'm going to do at the Agnews without a cat to keep me company. Lolly never loved me. That's why she's putting me away." She brought Worthy closer to her face so that she could wipe her nose with the back of her hand.

Mr. Stevens sat down on the rocker. He closed the flask and removed the gloves. He took his blue handkerchief from his breast pocket and wiped his brow. It was hot in Round Valley, nearly one-hundred degrees every day in the last week of August.

"Mrs. Hanson, you sure you can't take Worthy with you?"

"The Agnews said no and the railroad too. And I can't leave him here. You're leaving soon too, else I'd have asked you to take him for me.

"The dog pound would of done the same thing for Worthy. That's why I asked you to do it. I know it's hard. But I owe it to Worthy. He's been a good cat, and I can't bear to leave him, knowing the coyotes or Smith kids will get him." Her voice was shaky but she willed the tears from falling down her cheeks. Her face was set and her mind made up.

"All right, let's get this thing over with," Mr. Stevens said. He stood up, put the gloves back on, and opened the flask. He soaked the gauze and attached it to a hook inside the airtight container. He removed three sardines wrapped in a kerchief from his hip pocket and placed them on the floor of the container.

"Good thinking, Mr. Stevens. You know Worthy just loves those little fish." Mrs. Hanson put the cat on the card table, letting him find the fragrant fish. When he was inside, Mr. Stevens shut the door.

"Now we monitor Worthy. To make sure," he said. He took a breath and opened a long, metal flap on the side of the container that revealed a rectangular piece of glass soldered to the surrounding metal.

"To make sure everything goes all right, we can watch

him from this side. Just look through the glass, that's all."
Mrs. Hanson nodded and stooped next to Mr. Stevens to
see inside. Worthy was engrossed in the sardines, oblivious
to the tasteless and odorless gas.

"Won't take too long, I can assure you, Mrs. Hanson."
Then the tabby stopped eating. Worthy could no longer
stand. The cat lay on his side but struggled to get back up.
He held his head for as long as he could manage until he let
it fall, hitting the bottom of the container.

"He's still breathing, I can see his chest move," Mr.
Stevens said.

Worthy raised his head one more time to look out the
glass. His paws quivered and the orange-and-white fur bristled. Mrs. Hanson held her breath. Maybe Worthy wouldn't
die after all. Maybe the gas hadn't worked. She felt momentarily hopeful.

Then Worthy's head jerked back, and his body con-
vulsed and shook. Mrs. Hanson shuddered. His head thun-
ked one final time and, along with it, his slender frame
stopped shaking. He was dead.

Mr. Stevens put his calloused hand on Mrs. Hanson's
back, pulled one of the rocking chairs over, and gently sat
her in front of the table. He walked down the steps and
around back to give her some time alone with Worthy.

"If only I could have stayed on, we could have lived here
until we died," Mrs. Hanson said. "I would have struggled,
but I'd have made it all right. Instead, I was told to 'Git' and
git's what I'm doing. I'm leaving today, Worthy."

The sun was getting high, so Mrs. Hanson rose from the rocking chair, wiped her cheeks with her apron, swung open the screen door, and went inside for her hat. She ran her hands along the empty walls inside the house. Then she unfastened her apron and tossed it in a bin. *No cooking where I am going*, she thought. She marched straight through to the parlor, opened the window that looked out on the cottonwoods, and watched Mr. Stevens dig a hole. Now she was ready.

The Parable of the Pupfish

Julius had taken a leave of absence. He wasn't sure how long it would take or even if the outcome would include his wife's saving. A part of him knew he was going to return to work in due time as a widower. Another part thought the doctors might discover a miracle cure and they'd be lucky, extremely lucky.

He fantasized about the moment when an efficient nurse approached him to say that Irma was gone. He yearned for the relief and certainty of it. And that pulled him back to the waiting room. He shouldn't be thinking of himself, only of Irma. Only of her schedule, the medicines, the appointments, the long wait. Of how she would have done the same for him were he in this situation. He would not cogitate on the relief. He would turn to duty. To what was right. But no matter how often he chastised himself, he couldn't stop the conclusion that it wasn't fair, his wife dying at fifty-five. He resented her being lost in the folds of her nonfunctioning cerebral cortex. Did he resent her? No. It wasn't her fault that she inherited a brain disorder.

Inyo County Hospital was quiet. Guess no big emergencies happen on a Tuesday at eleven a.m., Julius thought. He dragged his foot back and forth across the linoleum and took in the speckles on the floor, attempting to discern a pattern. He tried to read the *Life* magazine, but it fell apart in his hands, and he didn't have the energy to retrieve the pages that had floated beneath the chairs. That's when Billy Haddard entered.

"Julius, come here, I want you." A real Bell-to-Watson moment. Billy was short of breath and covered in sweat.

"For what?"

"I figured I'd find you here."

"Billy, you okay?"

"Those assholes at Fish and Game won't listen. I need you to help me."

"Billy, I can't leave. You know that. I'm busy."

"Don't look busy. Besides, Irma won't know you're gone, and we only have a couple of hours at most." Julius couldn't argue with Billy. Irma had long ago stopped recognizing him.

"What are you in a rush about?"

"Pupfish."

"Okay, but let me tell the doctors."

"No time, and anyways, I just saw them all at lunch. So they don't need you. I need you." Julius put his mesh cap on and unfolded himself from the plastic lobby chair. Outside the hospital, he walked into a wall of heat. He wondered if his heart missed a beat or two.

"You sure you need me? I am pretty useless in this weather," Julius said. "Useless in general," he muttered to himself.

"Positive."

In Billy's truck, the vinyl upholstery burned against Julius' hands, and though he really should have put a towel down, he welcomed the sensation against his thighs. At least he could feel something, unlike Irma.

"I should be finishing the trout-management plan. But I snuck out to look at the pupfish. They're just barely hanging on."

"Water's going to evaporate. What equipment do we have?" Julius asked.

"Three buckets, some aerators, and a few nets. I also brought those wire-mesh cages that you like."

At the junction of Highway 6 and Highway 395, Billy took a right and floored it to Fish Slough, toward what could best be described as halfhearted puddles containing the last of the Owens Valley pupfish, a two-inch-long silver fish whose charisma—which is to say, its lack thereof—did not endear it to the average valley resident. It wasn't a sport fish, it wasn't edible, and it made no one any money. Not a cent.

Billy drove as close to the water holes as the cattails and wire grass would allow. Julius climbed out of the passenger side and grabbed a bucket and a net. He stepped over the sedges and around the cottonwood tree standing so starkly, alone against the desert sky. *I'm getting too old for this*, he thought. *Or maybe sitting in chairs for months on end, waiting on news that never seems to come, is wrecking me.*

It was worse than he thought. How many dead? Two, three, five hundred? The water was stale, ripe. He dipped his bucket in, filling it with half-alive fish. When it was full, he ran back to the truck. Billy attached an aerator to the bucket and fresh oxygen circulated.

"I am getting eaten alive out here."

"Bad year for mosquitoes," Billy said, slapping his arm as if to punctuate the point. He addressed the flat, thin insect smeared across his hot skin. "You'd already be dead if these waters had any pupfish left."

"Give me the other ones," Julius said, motioning for the other two buckets. He grabbed them and loped back to the pathetic collection of water. He filled them up with fish, both dead and alive. A sharp pain coursed through his lower back. He set the fish down to catch his breath and tried not to weigh the absurdity of this mission. *I am carrying fish that may go extinct in the next five minutes. I cannot trip. I cannot drop these buckets. Please God, get me back to the pickup.* When he completed his errand, Billy added the aerators.

"Hey, you okay? I could carry those," Billy said.

"Feels good to be useful, even if I look like these fish, like I'm going to die," Julius said. Billy patted him on the back, too young to appreciate the body of a fifty-seven-year-old man. Billy began a quick census.

"I estimate 850 here, Julius."

"Let's get them to a safer spot," Julius said, jumping into the bed of the truck before Billy drove to the main channel of the slough. Julius watched the pupfish dart irregularly about the plastic buckets. They were amazingly hardy fish, living in shallow water in the desert at temperatures of ninety and above; in winter, they lived below a couple inches of ice at air temperatures below zero degrees. But now, swimming in confusion and stressed beyond their natural tolerance, the pupfish flipped sideways and belly up.

Julius hit his fist on the windowpane of the cab. "Faster! I've got fish croaking back here!" Billy's old Chevy kicked up dust as he accelerated toward the spring source.

When they arrived, Julius barked orders. "Take this cage! Put it in the water and I'll bring the buckets." The water was less than four inches deep, but it was enough. Julius gently poured the fish into the cage. Julius and Billy stood and stared down at the small refuge.

"Will it work?" Billy asked. Julius shrugged his shoulders.

"Sometimes I wonder why we even try," he said.

"Don't know. Programmed to?" Billy said.

"That's probably right," Julius said and then sent Billy to Joseph's for sandwiches. As the Chevy pulled away, Julius walked toward a willow tree to take a piss. When he returned, he looked down to see that the cage no longer benefited from enough water. More fish belly up. Now that he was alone, he would have to work even faster, so he grabbed a net and began to transfer fish back into the buckets and then turned the aerators on. He jogged up the channel, looking for a better spot of water with more oxygen flow. When he found one, he ran back to the buckets, picked one up at a time, and returned, moving carefully around rodent holes and uneven terrain, his body imbalanced by the heavy load. He repeated the sequence three times. At the end of the transfer, at least a couple hundred more fish were dead.

He had so little time. "Just the cage now; have to get it in place," he said out loud, feeling the sharpened path of sweat careening down his chest and forehead. Then one of the aerator batteries died. A quick calculation—would more fish live or die if he ran for the cage? He decided to combine the three buckets into two. There would be less oxygen, but some was better than none.

He ran back to the first water hole and grabbed the cage. His throat was dried out from the heat, and he suddenly remembered his canteen in the Chevy.

Damn, why did I let Billy go? I need him, Julius thought. *Hold on there little guys!* He ran again to the new water hole with the cage. Kneeling, he emptied the two buckets into the cage, picking out the bodies of the dead fish and saying words Irma would have hated hearing, words that started with S and F. When he was done, he rose and stepped to a nearby cottonwood's shade. He doubled over, wheezed in what breath he could.

If only he could tell Irma about this day. She would chuckle and tell Julius how no one but him could love a

fish so small. And he'd reply that they were poor little bas-
tards who used to own the Owens River. These fish, he'd
say, once had so much room to grow, mature, and repro-
duce. Hell, the females might seek out their special fellas as
much as two hundred times a day! He'd pat her thigh and
wink. Then he'd tell her how the pupfish began losing their
water to the City. To make matters even more catastrophic,
the City introduced bass and trout that were hundreds of
times bigger, and stronger, than the pupfish. Those little
fish didn't run or cower, Irma. They were stubborn, territo-
rial buggers. They were too dumb to see the long odds they
faced at just two inches long—the game fish were fourteen
inches of killing and cunning. Of course the pupfish lost.
Irma would have cackled again. That's my Julius, saving
what no one else could care less about.

The boss would not be pleased about this. Two months
ago, he had told Julius to get his priorities straight.

"Julius, I don't have time to send you to Fish Slough to
watch over some little fish. Your trout-management program plan is your number-one job, and I have yet to see a
first draft," he had said.

"I understand that, but if we don't do something
soon, we're going to lose them permanently." The boss had
grunted and turned his back to Julius to file some paper-
work in a putty-colored cabinet.

"I just wonder, Julius, what the fuss is about. What
good are those fish anyway? They don't bring anglers from
Los Angeles. They don't make the hotels, the grocers, the

pack outfits any money. They don't do a lot, if you ask me." Julius had noticed the boss' blue button-down shirt stained by rings of sweat around the armpits. The conversation, it seemed, was over. Julius had returned to his desk to type up his management plan.

Now, in the late afternoon heat in the middle of a desert wetland, Julius knew what he would say next time. He straightened his spine, stood to look at the horizon, and heard the Chevrolet returning. A gentle gust of wind blew across the slough, moving the grass in unison and cooling his skin. He walked back to the cage and looked down at the pupfish. All were alive. The pupfish were calmer and, despite their entrapment, swam gracefully within the cage. Billy parked and hopped down.

"You moved them again?"

"Had to. Not enough circulation in the first spot."

"Shoot, I would have helped you. But I guess there wasn't enough time."

"It's all right. Impossible to know these things when they're happening."

"I guess. Well, Joseph's had your favorite cranberry-turkey sandwich. I brought some beers to celebrate too."

Julius pulled the tab on the can of Coors and raised it high. He looked at Billy, who was devouring his roast beef sandwich. *Young, energetic, and good in a pinch*, Julius thought, biting into the most delicious sandwich in the valley and glancing down at the cage that contained the last of a kind. The cranberry was juicy and sweet in his dry mouth.

He shut his eyes and in his mind rehearsed his line. *You ask what good the pupfish are to us. Well, I ask, what good are you to them?*

When Julius returned to the office, he'd tell the boss what was what, that the Owens River pupfish could have been lost forever. But for now, there they were, swimming in the brown water, safe in their part of the universe.

"Shit."

"What?" Billy asked.

"Oh, nothing. Didn't mean to say that. Nothing at all." Julius wouldn't tell the boss anything. But he would tell Irma. She would understand. It would matter to her, even though the real Irma was buried in the sedimentary layers of her damaged mind. He imagined her sitting up, looking into his eyes, reaching for his hands and bringing them to her lips, shaking her head, and having a good laugh at his expense. It would feel good. Really good.

The Girl's a Bore

Dusty planned each scene with the precision of an army general, attuned to safety, to the horses' comfort, to the director's needs, to the placement of the actors, to the cinematographer's litany of complaints. Rarely did he need more than two takes. He saved the producer money just by walking on the set.

"Wish I could find ten more like him," Mr. Deane said to the producer. "Best stuntman I've ever had. Saved me a bundle on the last picture after that scuffle with the Navajos. They wanted me to hire all *their* horsemen. Would have cost me a fortune. Dusty talked them out of it somehow. Handled all the horse runs himself and not one horse was lost."

"Except for that pony, Mr. Deane," said the assistant, who was taking notes and wasn't supposed to talk. Mr. Deane shot him a look. The assistant looked down at his notepad.

"Like I said, no *horses* were lost on that set," Mr. Deane said. "Not a one. You can ask any wrangler that was there."

Forty years later Dusty is on a panel at a school gymnasium at the Lone Pine Film Festival, discussing "Stunt Design, Animal Husbandry, and Plot." Outside, festival attendees stroll from shop to shop or pause to take photographs with locals dressed as Wild Bill Hickok, Mae West, and John Wayne.

Dusty comes yearly to relive each frame of his stunt career, speaking in front of rapt audiences in love with a fictional past created by men beneath the sharp teeth of the Sierra. On this land, most of the stories are based on fantasies with three crucial elements—violent clashes with natives who look more like Lakota Sioux warriors than Paiutes, long-barreled guns and worn felt hats, and belles who are not only in distress but who know so little of their own desires that a man has to spell it out for them in a slow drawl.

Dusty draws the crowds, still slim in his Levi jeans and cowpoke cotton shirts with silver-pointed collars. Never married, Dusty has a gentle voice worn down by the yelping on the set. He is always accompanied by a lady friend who beams while he sits on the panels. He packs them in, eager Western enthusiasts, aging locals proud of their place in celluloid history, curious reporters sent by the *Los Angeles Times* and high desert newspapers, and television anchors.

And, this time, one woman named Hilda Rinehardt, who came to retrieve what was rightfully hers: her true love, her virginity, her youth.

Hilda walked into the back of the room, saw Dusty and several other stuntmen onstage, and sat down. Her entrance went unnoticed. The room went dark but for the stage lights. If Dusty could have seen who was in the audience, he would have recognized her. It was her long eyelashes, her thick and shiny hair, and, most of all, the ample curve of her bottom lip. He would have recalled the hours he spent nibbling, licking, and sucking on that bottom lip and the hours in his trailer with his hands under Hilda's blouse, cupping her breasts and feeling her quivering breath beneath him.

She sighed and let her mind wander to the moment when her time in Hollywood was undone. One of Dusty's men, an older teenager named Thomas Bent, was to dress as Hilda and sit sidesaddle while galloping a horse to a lookout. She had noticed how poorly Thomas rode. "I could do that better than him," she had told Dusty. Dusty refused. So she had withheld her favors the rest of the week. By Sunday, Dusty relented and allowed her to do her own stunt. Mr. Deane was furious. "Do that again, missy, and you'll see a pink slip the size of my ass." She had giggled. He banned her from the set for the next week with the exception of her scenes. Still, she hadn't thought much of it. She sulked in her trailer and did some knitting. At the end of her punishment, she promised Mr. Deane to be good. "Just be the actress I hired you to be—nothing more, nothing less," he had said. She nodded and kissed Mr. Deane on the cheek. He wiped his face. "Now get on," he said, nearly hitting her bottom with the back of his hand.

That's when she had made the mistake. Ignoring Mr. Deane's warning. *He's ornery, but I can handle him*, she had thought. *I'm not going to listen to what everyone says. I will go somewhere in this business on my own two feet, not because he makes it so.*

About three weeks after her expulsion and subsequent reentry to the set, Hilda told Dusty she would perform her own stunt during the biggest scene in the film.

The shot required four teams of six horses apiece, each pulling a wagon filled with props such as hay and mining supplies, and they would careen toward the edge of a cliff like they had a death wish. But Dusty would whistle and signal the teams to stop, seemingly just in time. Of course, in real life there would be plenty of time to stop. Only stunt doubles would be used, and only the fastest, youngest, most courageous horses would do. There were three women in the scene, and, of course, the stuntmen would play their body doubles.

"I can't let you do it, darling," Dusty said.

"Sure you can. You can do anything you like. You're his favorite."

"Mr. Deane would have my hide, you know that."

"Nah, he would never even know. How can he tell whether the body double is actually me riding? He'd be at least a hundred yards away."

"True."

"Think about it, Dusty."

"I'll think about it, but you aren't going to do it."

"Come on. You know I can do it. You've seen me ride." Dusty scooped Hilda into his arms and they fell back onto the bed.

"I'd like you to ride me."

"You sick man!" She loved his dirty talk.

"I'm sick in love's what I am," he said, turning suddenly serious.

"Yeah?"

"You bet. I love you, girl," he said, looking into her eyes for an answer.

"I loved you the moment I saw you."

"Would you consent to stay in love forever?"

"I would, except you love a lot of women from what I've heard," she said.

"Not anymore. What would you say right now if I got the Buick ready and we drove to Reno?"

"And?"

"And got ourselves a marriage license, some rings, and a honeymoon suite at the Silver Nugget?"

"Get married?"

"That's what I'm saying. Marry me, Hilda. Be my wife."

No one knew, since the entire crew had the weekend off, that Hilda married Dusty. And they decided to keep it secret until filming had concluded, just to keep things straight with Mr. Deane. Mr. Deane didn't care about the flirting and romping in the trailers, but he cared about professionalism and being on time and making sure everyone understood the chain of command. There was Mr. Deane and then there was everybody else.

If only Hilda had understood that simple fact. But even if she had, she would have done the same thing. Bucked the system, then been punished by it. But the punishment. It had been outsized, grandiose, and far crueler than the deed. Hadn't it? Hilda pulled a Kleenex from her purse. The panelists were adjusting their microphones. Dusty's microphone squealed and the audience covered their ears. Hilda blew her nose and shook her head. She had paid. Again and again, she had paid for her mistake.

The secretary had marched them to the office. Mr. Deane looked up from his clipboard.

"Now, Dusty Nolan, Hilda Rinehardt. What do the two of you have to say for yourselves?" Hilda looked at Dusty. His chin nearly touched his chest.

"Sir, I'm awfully sorry. I never meant for that animal to die. I didn't know it was rigged up that way. I'm not that kind of..." Hilda's face ran with tears.

"I'm not concerned about the horse there, Hilda. What I'm more upset about is that you thought you could be in the stunt. You're not a man! Hell, even if you were a man, you're not in the union. I could get big fines here!"

"Sir, I just thought," she began.

"You didn't think, and that's the problem, Hilda," Mr. Deane said.

"I thought I could do the stunt better than that young fellow. You see, I grew up on a ranch in Wyoming. Been riding my whole life. I know all about it."

"Enough. Dusty, the real question here is how this could have happened. You're my best stunt coordinator. You're one of the best riders. Jesus, you're one of the best employees here. And I am having a hard time believing Hilda's story. She told me you permitted her to do this. Is that correct?"

The airless office was quiet. Hilda could hear an Indian outside sweeping the patio beneath the awning, the broom's delicate straw brushing across the concrete pad Mr. Deane always laid down on the set. She turned to Dusty and tried to catch his eye.

"Mr. Deane, it's not Dusty's fault. I convinced him I could do it. I knew I could. And it would have worked but for the wires."

"Enough, Hilda. I'm talking to Dusty. Dusty, did you or did you not permit Hilda to do this stunt?"

"I did not." There, those were the three words. They hung like heavy wool pants drying on a clothesline, wet with animal sweat and saddle sore. He did not. He did not let her do this unthinkable thing. "She slipped onto the set while I wasn't looking, and because she's about the same size as Thomas Bent, I didn't recognize it was her."

"That's not true! Dusty, why are you lying?"

"Ain't lying. It's the absolute truth," Dusty said, his gaze avoiding Hilda's gaping mouth. Mr. Deane pressed a button on the intercom.

"Ruth, get security. Miss Hilda will be escorted back home. Have the driver take her to Mojave. She can arrange transportation from there. I want her removed as quickly as possible." Within moments, a man named Porty arrived and gently moved Hilda outside. "Sorry, miss" was all he said.

Porty dropped her off and handed her an envelope with enough cash for bus fare to Los Angeles. Before backing the company car out of the lot, he gave Hilda a sorrowful look. She waved. She hadn't even had time to pack her bags and find Dusty. Surely he would come after her. So she waited. The afternoon bus pulled up, but she did not get on it. She knew he was on his way. Dusty would run to her and beg her forgiveness. And she would give it to him. She would give him her affection, and he would find her another job— maybe on the television series he would start on after this picture wrapped up.

Another bus came before sunset, and she did not board.

"You sure, miss? Next bus ain't until tomorrow same time," the driver said. She shook her head. "Suit yourself," the man said. And she had. She waited all night in the cold bus shelter, and when it was past one o'clock in the morning, she began praying. At dawn, she rose from the bench to find a cup of coffee at the diner next door and then hitched a ride back to Los Angeles with a family.

Back in Hollywood, she threw herself into auditions. Each time it was the same. After she finished reading, an assistant would lean and whisper into the director's ear. Once, she heard the words "expelled by Deane." He had told every director about her. She couldn't even get a job as the toothpaste girl on a quiz show.

The picture would have made Hilda a star. It enjoyed the biggest budget of any Western ever made with all the big names—Stewart, Marvin, a young Eastwood, Grant. It would be filmed in Cinerama, a new technology for large theaters featuring interlocking, curved screens so that audiences would feel like they were there under the hot sun, riding hard, and chasing Indians between the rocky outcroppings of the Alabama Hills. You'd feel so close to the action that you could practically taste the dust from the horse in front of you.

"You're not really a leading lady, Hilda," Mr. Deane had told her. His first words. "Not in this picture. Maybe never. Not your strong suit."

"So what am I, then?"

"A foil."

"A foil?"

"Yeah, kind of a comic character. Minstrel, prostitute, something low like that. Will make the audience laugh. But not a leading lady, no, I wouldn't describe it that way."

"That's the way you described it to my agent."

"That was his interpretation."

"He told me you were looking for a woman who was feminine but tough, who could ride, hold a shotgun, bare a little cleavage, serve as a love interest, but also show a firm pioneer exterior. Nothing about being a prostitute or singer."

"Minstrel."

"Mr. Deane, you're belittling me."

"Look, Hilda, if you don't want the part, I got fifty women who do."

"Well, I'm here and ready to work. I'll do it. But next time, you tell my agent what you're really looking for. If it's a hooker you want, it's a hooker you'll get."

"I don't want a hooker. You play it that way and you're fired."

"But you just said you wanted a prostitute."

"Hilda, you got to understand. Whenever I bring the girl in, I got to make sure things don't come to a terrible stop. Because that's a tendency in Westerns, in any action picture. The girl is a bore." Mr. Deane turned, shouted to an assistant for another cup of coffee, and waved Hilda away.

The scene had been planned from every angle, marked up, walked through, and then ridden with the horses carefully, ploddingly gentle, haltingly, so that no horse was spooked. But when filming started, Dusty knew he was in for the biggest stunt of his life at $1,000 an hour for the wranglers, cameras, and dynamite.

At the tack barn before the scene, Dusty had supervised the preparations. More than once, he walked up to a wrangler who had whispered "Can't be done" under his breath. "We'll do it," Dusty had said. "You'll break the animal's neck," a wrangler said. "No, I won't. Now enough of that," Dusty had said and spat on the ground, narrowly missing the wrangler's boots.

Hilda's horse had its feet wired, and the wires were run up through the saddle and out. The horse was to get up a good run, and then the wrangler would jerk the wires and pull the horse's front feet out from under him.

She went over as planned, unhurt. But the horse didn't make it. He broke his neck. Dead at the end of the take. One stuntman fractured his pelvis. But the take was a good one and, as Dusty promised, it only had to be done the once.

The moderator asks the audience for questions. Hilda stands up.

"I had the fantasy of becoming the first stuntwoman in the union," she began. "I forced my way into a stunt and I let it ruin my life." The reporter from the *Times* wheeled around in his chair. The moderator looked up from his notepad.

"What's your name, then?"

"Hilda," she said.

"Are you Hilda Rinehardt? The actress fired by Farrington Deane for insubordination? I've been wondering for years where you went!" the reporter said. Hilda smiled, brushed a wisp of hair from her eyes, and bit her bottom lip.

"Been in Canada this whole time. A friend told me about this festival. I saw Dusty was here. So I came." Dusty grabbed at his breast pocket for a kerchief. He dabbed at his eyes and wiped his brow.

"All these years later, what do you think about that day you were fired?" the reporter asked.

"It wasn't very bright on my part. I was very naive. It was the last shot of the day. Mr. Deane was absolutely furious. The result was that I was banned from the set and fired. It was devastating to me. It haunted me for the rest of my life. I hadn't even started my career." She stared at Dusty. "I also lost my husband that day. He never came for me."

"Yes, I did," Dusty said. The reporter looked at Dusty and back at Hilda.

"You two were married?"

"Still are," said Dusty. The moderator fumbled with the soundboard and shut the microphones off. He rose and clapped his hands.

"Let's give our panelists a round of applause!" The reporter hurried to Hilda's side. Dusty stood, removed his hat, and held it over his chest. Hilda began walking down the aisle. By the time she reached him, tears rolled down her cheeks.

"I looked for you for so long, Hilda," Dusty said. "Even hired a private detective. He couldn't get any information out of anybody. One clue led him to Mexico. I paid him a lot of money, and all I got was a bottle of tequila." He pulled her close.

"I didn't want you to find me," she said.

"Why?"

"I couldn't face you."

"I don't blame you," Dusty said.

The reporter shouted, "Mr. Nolan, Miss Rinehardt, a photo please?"

"I changed my name and hitched to Vancouver. Been there ever since," she said. "I'm a retired math teacher."

"Got a family?"

"No, just a dead husband. When he passed away last June, I thought I ought to find you again."

"And here I am. You want an apology?" said Dusty.

"I do."

"Let's hop in my truck. I'll take you for a ride." The reporter and the rest of the audience watched as Hilda and Dusty walked out into the cool October morning.

"Still got that pretty lower lip, Hilda."

"I still got a lot of things."

"I'm sure you do." He noticed her shining fistfuls of hair and the long eyelashes.

"You lose weight, Dusty?"

"Yes, getting old. Don't jump from moving trains and horses anymore."

"Don't look old to me."

"You don't look a day older than when I met you." Dusty drove out Whitney Portal to Movie Flat Road, silent as he maneuvered around piles of rounded, shapely granite boulders brushed and refined by snow and wind. He stopped from time to time to point out the site of scenes he shot with her. When they arrived on the wide expanse of sandy plateau where the stunt had gone so horribly wrong four decades ago, he shut the engine off.

"What I did was cowardly and inexcusable. Selfish, malicious. I was wrong. Can I make amends?" Dusty asked.

Hilda looked down at the floorboards of the Dodge pickup. After several moments, she merely nodded.

"Good, good," he said and patted her on the knee. He wanted to say more than that, but the frog in his throat and his running nose prevented it. He blew his nose into his kerchief and then drove back into town, parking in front of the Pine Café. He suggested the biscuit and gravy special and Hilda nodded again.

After ordering, Dusty said, "Do you think what was lost can be regained?"

"You mean, can we have a happy ending? This isn't Hollywood, Dusty." He lifted the coffee mug to his lips. He did not know what to say. And when words hid from him, he heeded their power. He looked at Hilda, his eyes glassy.

"I just mean that I don't care about happy endings. Right now, the only thing I care about is beginnings," Hilda said. Words scarce and yet heavy all around him, Dusty began to cry.

"Do I deserve it?" he asked.

"Not a question of deserving," Hilda said. "I forgave you a long time ago."

"When you got married and moved on up to Canada?"

"No, when I waited for the bus back to Los Angeles, right after Farrington Deane fired me."

"That quick?"

"I don't hold grudges."

Dusty reached for Hilda's hands across the Formica tabletop.

"I don't know what to say, girl. You knocked me off my feet then. Doing it now too. With you in the picture, I am the luckiest man in the Owens Valley. Hell, the world."

"So the girl stays in the picture?" Hilda laughed. The waitress asked if they required anything else.

Dusty rose, kissed the waitress' hand, and placed a big bill into her palm. "Thanks, we got everything we need."

The Mounds of Mitsue

"You volunteered to drive us, you know," Grandma Mitsue said.

"I know. But maybe I shouldn't have."

"Keep two hands on the steering wheel, please," Grandma Mitsue said.

"Aye, aye, Captain," said Andrea.

"Don't tease me. This trip is important to me."

"I know, Obaa-san. Sorry."

The walking tour began in front of the Park Service visitor center and gift shop, a former school gym used by the internees that was visible from Highway 395. Her mother had said it was the perfect getaway. Forget about your husband (she didn't say "ex") for a little while, see something new, spend some one-on-one time with Obaa-san, and do a little gambling. "See your life in a new way. Think with a clear view," Mitsue had added. Mother and Obaa-san seemed to believe that Andrea just needed a little reflection time in order to recover from her divorce. It was awfully naive, but Andrea didn't say anything.

Mitsue moved well and did not yet need a walker or cane. She pressed in toward the Park Service ranger so that she could hear every word.

"What is your name and where are you from?" Mitsue asked. The round woman with full cheeks smiled broadly. Her teeth were straight and very white, her chest large, and her belt hooked on the last hole.

"My name is Heather Lovelace. I'm Paiute from Big Pine just forty-five minutes down the highway."

"Nice to meet you, Ms. Lovelace. I'm Mitsue Tanaka and I used to live here. I've not been back since 1944. I've brought my granddaughter and I intend to show her how it was to live here on this land. I never wanted to come before now."

Heather Lovelace nodded her head politely.

"I will caution all of you," Heather Lovelace began, "it's very cold outside. We will walk briskly but bundle up. It is good when it is hot or when it is cold—it reminds us how difficult it must have been to live under this sun without air conditioning and in this winter climate with only the clothing brought from San Pedro. On top of all that, not knowing when you would be allowed to go home."

Andrea already wanted to go home. She had heard Mitsue's stories over the years and wasn't keen to see the place where her Soba, her grandmother, had lived during the war. Mitsue had told about how her father was taken by the FBI, followed by the rest of Mitsue's family's evacuation from Terminal Island. She told her about the prized Victrola left and the fishing boat her father had partly owned also left behind. Mitsue had listed what was confiscated—tackle, nets, poles . . . in fact, any and all of the businesses built by the Issei. Their belongings were never returned, and their homes on Terminal Island were wiped from the map, every home destroyed, the mom-and-pop grocer on Tuna Street cleaned out, shut up, shut out.

The Manzanar barracks were not winterized—slits between the wood planks let the alkaline dust and snow enter. There was a riot at one point. Some boys died. Andrea half listened to these tales. She could hardly resolve her own problems, much less confront Mitsue's difficult past. She tried to think about tomorrow, when she would be seated in front of a slot machine and drinking beers alongside old women smoking. Secretly, she enjoyed the cheerless rooms of small casinos filled with people who were really too poor to play. It made her feel slightly superior, as though she wasn't as bad off as the locals with their puckered skin, cancer-ridden wrinkles, and bad teeth. Plus, Mitsue would be so busy playing the machines that she wouldn't question Andrea too much; Mitsue would be engulfed in winning a dollar here, a quarter there.

"Andrea, you have the camera?" Mitsue wanted to show pictures of the grounds to her friends at the senior center. She wanted to prove she had done it, that she went back to acknowledge her suffering, Andrea guessed. Mitsue would gather a few pebbles, rub the fine sand between her finger-tips, and stare at the shoulders of the giant mountains that had guarded her—or confined her—so many years ago.

Andrea pulled the digital camera from her tote bag and placed the strap around her neck. She didn't care if she looked like a Japanese tourist. Hell, she pretty much *was* a Japanese tourist, she thought as she walked behind Mitsue's petite frame.

"We're going to the gatehouse first," Heather Lovelace announced. Mitsue stared down and wiped her nose with the back of her freckled hand.

"Obaa-san, are you okay? Is this going to be too difficult?"

"Yes, mago, it's going to be what it is. Today is the day to see and to go back."

"It wasn't that bad, was it? I mean, it wasn't a real concentration camp." Andrea handed Mitsue a couple of tissues. They followed Heather Lovelace in silence.

"We weren't gassed, no. But there was barbed wire. It was a camp, and we couldn't leave. We didn't know why Roosevelt turned on us like that," Mitsue finally said. Heather Lovelace saved Andrea from a reply.

"Notice the gatehouse is made of large rocks from the nearby hills. It's volcanic and came out of the ground during the last eruptions, maybe ten thousand years ago. Any geologists in the group? No? Well, geologists always have a good time in the Owens Valley. History buffs, too. Anyone know where the name of this camp came from?"

Mitsue smiled. "Named for the Spanish word for apple, *manzana*."

"Yes, ma'am. Hard to believe, but there were once apple orchards here. This whole valley was once full of green— apples, pears, alfalfa, grapes."

"What happened?" Andrea asked.

"Growers came to the valley when water was plentiful, but the orchards died in the early 1920s and 1930s when water from the Owens River was diverted and families abandoned or sold their land."

A man with a gray Stetson hat pulled up to the gate- house in a well-used pickup truck.

"Hello Rod," Heather Lovelace waved. "Right on time. Just getting my tour going." She smiled, shook his hand, and then turned to the group, winking.

"Miss Lovelace," Rod said, tipping his hat to her and to the others, "I come every Saturday to do my protesting. Maybe you all will stop after and take my brochure. This place is a sham and ought to be commemorating veterans of the war, not people who were inconvenienced. My Pop died in the war and that was a mighty hardship for my mother, who raised me all alone in Big Pine. But the Park Service gone and put the welcome mat out for the Japs. But Miss Lovelace is like her name, lovely, and I am sure you'll have a nice tour. I'll see you folks later."

Heather Lovelace gestured toward the mountains. "Let's walk." She waited a few moments before laughing.

"I love Rod. Got a belief and nothing's going to change

it. My people deserve a monument too. You could say we've been inconvenienced the longest. We were marched down to Fort Tejon in 1863, even the old women. We were chased down to Owens Lake, where we were raped, shot, and killed. We were falsely accused. Like a windstorm, blown off our land, forced into the hills and mountains. Later, we became servants to the whites. But Rod's got his history, and I've got mine."

"Why aren't your people protesting?" Mitsue asked.

"I guess we're just used to things the way they are. This land was ours for thousands of years. But not since the Spanish missionaries and the settlers came. No, we know that change is the way, not the exception. We lost something, but the whites did too. They lost their farms, their way of life. And us, well, we eat white people food now. See," she said, as she patted her layer of soft jelly overflow from her leather Park Service belt. She laughed again and stopped at marker nine. This, she said, was where some of the Terminal Islanders lived. She reached into a tote bag and pulled out a dozen laminated photocopies of what they could no longer see—the flimsy wooden barracks, lined one next to the other, brutish, serious, simple, and uninspired.

"You remember yours, ma'am?" Heather Lovelace asked Mitsue, who nodded. "What many Japanese-Americans have told me is that they wanted to be American. Their children were born in the United States, raised here, and they learned English and adopted American ways. But they were not considered citizens."

"Grandma, where did you live?" Andrea asked, as if the information were just a piece of mundane personal history, like her birth date or the color of her eyes. Mitsue stepped away toward sagebrush, a plastic grocery bag blowing across the desert over some weathered silver branches.

"Aren't you going to answer me?" Andrea turned toward Heather Lovelace. "Just let her do her thing, I guess."

Heather Lovelace continued. "When the camp was here, it was the largest city in the valley. To this day, it has remained the largest in the valley's history. Now, the biggest population's in Bishop. But even that's small, about thirty-five hundred people. That's where the largest Paiute reservation is located. And for you gamblers, there's a casino right on Highway 395. Isn't much compared to Reno, but it gives our community some money," Heather Lovelace said.

Mitsue continued walking.

"I better follow her," Andrea said. "Obaa-san, where are you going?"

"Just looking."

"Looking at what? There's nothing here."

"You can't see it, but I can. This way to the hospital."

They continued along the dirt road lined by naked willow trees. Andrea noticed a colorful Buzz Lightyear figurine, probably dropped during an elementary class field trip. Bits of bone, an eyeglass lens, and a few pennies littered the ground. When they reached marker number twenty, Andrea paused, taking stock of the square stones, gopher holes, and frozen water in the garden pond. She tried to see the hospital and the morgue buildings as they were, but everywhere she looked she was surrounded by mere suggestions and gray outlines. Concrete slabs from foundations, silhouettes from the knotted and craggy trees, small and medium sized pebbles dispersed by time, and a descending concrete channel that once carried water from a miniature mythical mountaintop down to a pool below. It took a lot to recreate the sense that ten thousand people once lived here in an organized fashion. She saw dozens of smaller stones that had been deposited by visitors in piles, as well as strings of paper cranes and colored glass.

"Andrea-chan, this is where I lost everything one day in May."

"What do you mean?"

"I was in this hospital for two months."

"What did you have?"

"It's what I didn't have. I lost my baby girl."

"But I thought you met Ojii-san after the war."

"I nearly bled to death. But I was lucky." Mitsue's knees buckled and she fell sidelong onto the granite slabs of the hospital's foundation. It happened so quickly that Andrea could not prevent Mitsue's hip from hitting and shattering against the hard stone.

"Andrea-chan," Mitsue said. Her eyes rolled backward, her eyelids fluttered, and then she fainted. Heather Lovelace radioed for help. Within fifteen minutes, the sheriff from Independence had pulled up to offer Mitsue, who had regained consciousness, a ride to the hospital in Bishop.

In the back seat of the sheriff's car, Mitsue was still on the stone steps of the hospital, her mind years away, in labor on an early summer afternoon on a simple bed covered in dampened sheets, a white doctor unable to save her daughter. They didn't give your stillborn baby a grave.

Andrea cradled her grandmother and shielded her face from the sun. The sheriff had turned on his siren.

"Mago, I killed her with my mind. I didn't want her born in the camp. I willed her to die."

"Shh, Obaa-san, we're almost to Bishop. You did nothing wrong. You're going to be fine." Andrea rocked Mitsue and rested her lips on her grandmother's scalp.

"I don't want to die here," Mitsue said. "Not like my daughter."

"Obaa-san, it's just your hip, no big deal," Andrea said. "Anyways, she was never born, she doesn't exist."

Mitsue was back in the Manzanar hospital barrack in 1944 with the doctors and nurses, the new parents, the aging, and the dying. From her window she notices one heavy, ripe Winesap apple about to drop. She imagines picking it, wiping it off on her pant leg, taking a bite, and tasting the sweet, crispy flesh. She hears the irrigation ditch water encircling a cottonwood. She knows the ground is moist about the base of the tree. She can see its leaves from her bed; they strike a confident green against the midday light that has washed away the colors of the granite mountains. Children play a made-up game in the distance. A white English teacher, age twenty-two, sits by her side, holding her hand. His eyes are reddened and glassy with tears. He has brought her the Winesap. He tells her he will marry her someday, after the war is over. She shakes her head. "Can never happen." She rises despite her weak muscles, walks to the door, and throws the apple into the desert.

Mitsue opened her eyes to a harsh halo of light. She could hear Andrea barking orders.

"You just relax, Obaa-san, they're finding you a doctor," Andrea said. But Andrea was worried. She noted Mitsue's gray eyes looked cloudy, her pupils dilated.

"They say the hospital has one of the best hip replacement surgeons in the Sierra." Andrea wished she had never agreed to drive Mitsue to this godforsaken place. *I will not lose my grandmother over a stupid fall on stupid ground in the stupid desert.* Perhaps Rod is right. What kind of government makes a park out of a place that hardly exists? Just the demarcations of where buildings once stood, numbered wooden posts, panels with photographs of how it was, dead fruit trees, a white obelisk claiming to be soul-consoling, and headstones of half a dozen dead at the base of Mount Williamson. Nothing to celebrate or commemorate.

Driving alone down Highway 395 two months later, Andrea steadied her gaze on the dotted lines of the highway and counted the power transmission towers. Soba wanted her ashes placed next to her long-dead husband's in Long Beach. Andrea wanted a small portion to spread at Manzanar. To be near Mitsue's stillborn baby. If Andrea drove fast enough, she would arrive in Lone Pine by sunset.

She checked into the Dow Villa and got back in the car. The gate to Manzanar had not yet closed. Andrea pulled in, noticed the parking lot was empty, and decided to drive to the camp hospital. She had the road to herself. When she reached the cottonwoods with the ghostly garden and its frozen pond, she pulled a Ziplock bag from her pocket. She chose a patch of sand and dug a small hole with a stone, emptied the ashes out, and sat on her knees. The air was silent and the highway still. Rabbits hopped among the sagebrush.

"I didn't want to let you go here. You should have been in Long Beach. Not here. This isn't your home. This wasn't the right place to die." She began to cry. She didn't hear Heather Lovelace's pickup truck.

"No place is ever the right place," Heather Lovelace said, leaning out the window.

"Sorry, don't mean to loiter. I'm leaving."

"Stay, stay. You need to say good-bye. I'll leave you be. I just wanted to say again how sorry I am. Hip replacement surgery happens all the time. I'm sorry for your loss."

"She caught an infection and couldn't fight it off. Hospitals are the last place you want to be when you are sick, apparently." In the distance, a freight truck's horn sounded. "Now I have lost something at Manzanar too. Just like my Grandma."

"You know, Indians have sayings about these mountains and bushes and even the rocks and concrete foundations.

Spirit can be in all of them. I would say that's why you're here. Your grandma's spirit is here. Bet all the others are here too. She's with friends now. I know it doesn't help much now but sometime it will. You can always come back to visit."

"That sounds like a load of New Age bullshit," Andrea said.

Heather Lovelace laughed. "Yeah, but we Indians had that bullshit going before the New Age movement got a hold of it. Take it or leave it." Heather hopped down from the truck and squatted next to Andrea. She placed her forefinger on the small mound where the ashes were buried.

"Only thing we know for sure is change."

"Yeah, this is sure going to be a change," Andrea said.

"Now, you have a new, different life. Your family too. Only thing you can depend on, I guess. Well, you come by the visitor center and see me next year." Heather Lovelace grunted as she straightened her legs. Andrea listened for the truck to pull away. When she was absolutely sure she was alone, she sobbed into the sandy ground, aware that the sun had gone behind the mountains and that this small spot in the middle of nowhere was suddenly hers. The Sierra's long shadows came over her and the ash mound and continued across to the east where the Inyo Mountains still glowed. In between two great uplifts in the earth, Andrea kneeled, not to say good-bye but to wonder how she would get up and go.

Of course I will get back in the car, she thought, *and drive back to the motel and then drive back to LA. Then go back to work, back to my divorce, back to all of the things in Soba's house*. She took a breath but remained on the ground. She placed her palm over the mound and closed her eyes.

A strong gust of warm wind came suddenly across the grounds, knocking her backward. She caught herself with her hands, scrambled to right herself, and then turned to see a whipping funnel of sharp, sandy particles about ten feet high careening toward the north firebreak. *Dust devil*, she thought. *Or the spirits of Mitsue's fellow internees and her stillborn baby? Maybe the spirits in the stones, the sage, and the trees that Heather Lovelace and her people know?*

She looked down at where the ash mound had been. *Damn, took Soba away.* It felt poetic and yet terrible that nature, or the spirits, or whatever, didn't much care for Mitsue's body or Andrea's need to see it safely harbored. She shook her head. In the morning, things would be seen in a new light, and clarity would come, just as Soba always said. What else could be done tonight? The hospital's garden pool and granite stairs were no longer visible in the moments between sunset and moonrise. Andrea thought about the answer—*Nothing. For now, nothing.*

Elvis

A forest ranger is about to be contacted by a tree. Yes, a tree, *Pinus longaeva*, an old, undersized specimen commonly known as the bristlecone.

John Regent pauses on a trail in the White-Inyo Mountains, miles above the Owens Valley in a four-thousand-year-old bristlecone-pine forest. He gazes across the nearly barren terrain to the road below, where a snaking line of cars is making its way toward the visitor center. His colleague, Rhoda, is working the front desk and will say to visitors, as they say every day, that they cannot divulge to anyone the location of the park's oldest tree. Privately, they call that bristlecone "Elvis" since this tree is the king, handsome as the younger Elvis, branches wide as the older Elvis' collars, and bark as black as the boy from Tupelo's hair.

"Went up to see Elvis on my lunch break," Rhoda would say, or "I took a short nap under Elvis this afternoon," John would say, or "Some kids started heading up to Elvis, but turned around when their mother yelled," Rhoda would say. It was not easy to get to Elvis but with good hiking boots and a little awkward scrambling over the rocky face of its location, it was certainly possible. But you had to know the way.

The bristlecone-pine forest bears witness to some two hundred generations of humanity—American Indians, Spanish missionaries, eastern-seaboard explorers, hikers, miners, soldiers, park rangers, homesteaders from the Midwest, and water seekers from Los Angeles County. All have roamed the forest's gnarled forms, finding trees stunted and twisted by the wind and cold, tattooed by fire and lightning, and hardened into wise, ponderous, and seemingly impervious beings. These trees link the Babylonians, pharaohs, and nomadic tribes of the Far East to the loud, show-off, think-they're-so-cool young women and men who no doubt will get high up here, where the air is cooler than in the valley and where they can feel the mystery of the trees. John couldn't help but acknowledge that kids with attitudes could have spiritual experiences with the trees just as much as he did every day. The trees did not discriminate; in fact, they shared their accumulated wonder with anyone who paid attention.

John climbed to Elvis, the visitor center now out of view and the surrounding pines obscuring his ascent. Elvis was well protected and enjoyed a commanding station on the back side of the slope. John sat and unwrapped his sandwich, enjoying the summer warmth and a patch of sunlit ground near Elvis' trunk. He glanced at his watch. Only fifteen more minutes of lunch break, and then he would return to the center to lead a 1:30 interpretive walk. The air was calm, only mountain bluebirds moving. Ground squirrels sunned themselves nearby. Beneath the branches, John took a deep breath. He was lucky, awfully satisfied with this life and with this ample turkey and cheese sandwich, thankful for his socks that prevented blisters, and grateful to the mountains, which appeared different with every glance. *Every day*, he thought, *every day I get to come here for work*. He took a bite.

The tree's first attempt to contact John was a dismal failure. Trees know well that humans do not credit so much as a shred of emotion to animals that are practically kin, let alone to vegetation. Most trees, when push came to shove, would never ask a man to acknowledge their sentience, but Elvis was different, hopeful even. He wanted to try. So Elvis reached down with the thin tip of a narrow branch and scraped it against John's left shoulder. John started.

Must have been a bird diving down, must have seen my shiny nameplate, John thought. There was a way to explain everything. He returned to his lunch.

Again, a tap, a gentle touch. No breeze, no birds— just John and the tree. *I did not sleep well last night. I'm tired. Need to get back to work.* John stood up and shoved the wrapper in his pack. *I'll just have a quick swig of water before heading back down*, he thought. *And I'll need to put on a little sunscreen.* He remembered to put a dab on the top ends of his ears, the vulnerable cartilage that he often neglected and found reddened in the mirror at night.

"Well, Elvis, got to run. You be good." John patted the trunk, swung his pack over his shoulder, and pulled out a stick of Wrigley's gum. As he opened the foil, he felt warm air on his neck and heard first a low rumble and then the whisper of a command.

"Die. Make me die."

He turned. "Who is saying that?"

"I am."

John scrambled around the tree, peered over the ledge, and saw nothing. Those college kids, he remembered. Must be a prank.

It was time to return. Rhoda would be eager to eat her lunch. John would keep busy with the guided walk and then with selling some natural history books to tourists and answering questions about tree-ring dating. He would sweep the wooden floors and perhaps even Windex the windows. He would stay occupied, would put in a few extra minutes, and then would drive directly to Big Pine that night and buy a six-pack from the gas station. He would drink at least three beers, and then he would eat at the coffee shop from a plate heaped with French fries and would even walk to the city park and feed the geese. Then he would hop back into his truck and drive back up the mountain, where he would lift weights and do his sit-ups and jump rope for as many minutes as he could stand it. And then, only then, would he go to bed. He would sleep soundly in the dead quiet of the park.

He would not hear the squirrels, their thin nails scratching on the roof of the cabin, and he would not awaken when the Steller's jays called. He would sleep until the last possible moment, and he would go into work refreshed. Surely, after a long night's sleep, he would find that Elvis was just as he always was, an old tree on an old mountain in a very remote place in the world, a tree that did not touch, talk, or make unreasonable requests. A tree, just a tree, with stunted branches growing twisted in the alpine winds; a tree stately and calming, clinging to the ground with tenacity, graciousness, and an elegance that was lacking in the valley far below.

"Some kids found Elvis," Rhoda said at lunchtime the next day. "They didn't know it though. They actually thought the tree above it was the oldest. Took some pictures and that was it. I told them they were nowhere near the oldest tree, but they didn't believe me," she said. "You have time to go up there? Just to check to make sure they didn't do anything?" John agreed.

John Regent found a yellow granola-bar wrapper near the tree above Elvis. Then he saw the damage. A primitively scratched heart with some couple's initials. Goddamned kids, proving their love by hurting a tree. He moved his fingertips over the heart and suddenly heard "Die. Help me die." Again, a warm burst of air, a clear, coherent voice, unmistakably Elvis. John turned toward the source of the voice.

"Jesus Christ, stop it!" He knew he sounded weak, ridiculous, scared.

"Die. Want to die. Please help me die."

"I don't know what the hell you want from me, but you must go away. I don't talk to ghosts, or voices, or whatever you are." John Regent made his stand. He wouldn't take this command, wouldn't give it credence. "I'm leaving. I'm going back to work."

"Please. I'm so tired. I just want to die." John played along. Whoever created this stunt was going to an awful lot of trouble.

"Why?"

"Seen too much. Tired. Awful tired. Want to go home."

"Home to where?"

"My home. You don't know it. I want to go soon."

"And how on earth do you expect me to kill you?"

"You know the ways."

"Well, I do know about forest fires," John said, hoping his sarcasm would somehow deflate the prankster's script.

"Mmm, yes."

"Hasn't been one here in decades. Not enough fuel."

"Quite right."

"There's always the chain saw."

"It would end quickly."

"Or poison, or a pest."

"A bit of suffering, then?"

"But you know that's all against the law, I hope?" For the first time, John thought the perpetrator might actually be contemplating just this sort of crime. He couldn't believe his own stupidity. He must immediately call the district ranger and report it.

He ran, scrambled with some carelessness, and fell down the slope. He righted himself, removed the small rocks that dug into his palms, and slipped again, hurtling alongside a slew of cascading pebbles. All the while, the jokester continued to plead, "Please, please help me die."

John wondered whether he would roll into the visitor center or off the small cliff to the north. I am going to get very hurt, he concluded. But a wide branch swept the ground in front of his tumbling frame, halting him in a forceful but malleable embrace so that he found himself gasping for air in a wooden sling, an arm of sorts, with his eyes and mouth filled with dust. He turned his head to see what shelf had blocked his personal avalanche. Elvis.

"Look," Elvis said. John opened his eyes and attempted to lift his head to examine his scrapes, or worse, if he had broken anything, but he found it impossible to move anything. Yet he felt no pain. He took in a large quantity of air. "Calm now, calm," he repeated to himself. He closed his eyes. *How can I contact Rhoda?*

And what he saw then were cavalry soldiers on glistening horses galloping toward a brimming Owens Lake. Flocks of gulls departed the surface in terror, guns blasted at figures fleeing on foot. Who were they? John forgot that he needed to get back to the station. He marveled at the vision, more vivid than a movie, for he could smell the damp horse hair and hear the high-pitched wails of those running away. The soldiers rode all around him, through him, despite him. John Regent was on the ground, and on it he felt the heat of the desert and wiped his eyes of the invasive sand. A bugle was blaring and the cavalry were riding, stampeding this enemy, pounding them in murderous rhythm. A soldier aimed his gun, and down went a woman and a child. The woman, a young Paiute. The baby in her arms fell into the water. The Indians were being chased to the water to drown. The infant was not shot. It was drowned.

"No, stop this, I can't watch this, I don't want to be here! This joke is over!"

"I'm only trying to show you why I want to die."

"Why, because there is violence? There's also peace!"

"I don't know about that. Look." A tidy miner's cabin near the dolomite mine beneath the bristlecone-pine forest. It is dawn. Four large Indian men approach the door, knock it down, and slaughter the two white men inside. They throw the miners down a shaft, but only after having scalped them and nailed the thin blood-encrusted skin to the cabin door.

"You see only bloodshed!" John Regent cries.

"I don't know about that. I see what I see."

"For every wrong, there are thousands of rights!"

"I just want to go," Elvis says.

"You're cursed, that's all it is. You've not seen the good in this world."

"You can help me die."

"You're asking me to kill you? Don't you see the irony in that? I'm about the last person who would want to destroy a bristlecone. I live to protect you."

"Only you can take my life. I could hope for lightning

to strike, to bury me in electric flame, but that death is random and unlikely. That's why I make my request to you, John Regent."

"And what will you do if I don't?"

"You will, young friend, you will." John could move his head now, and as he pushed himself up, Elvis placed a different branch firmly on John's chest. "There, there is more to see."

John Regent lowered himself sidewise to the ground, supine again. He witnessed men with firearms shooting grizzlies until the bears were exterminated across the state. He saw a rancher murder what would now be called a mentally handicapped boy, a boy nearing manhood, a boy stroking a cow's neck as if the boy considered the cow a treasured pet, a Paiute teenage boy who the white man branded thief, a coyote-boy stealing his steer. John had read all the books about the Owens Valley, had watched the public-television documentaries, had even met many of the old-timers in Bishop who remembered the days before Los Angeles had diverted the river away from the ranches, the farms, the orchards, the dreams of many a settler and pioneer. But these visions of Elvis were more powerful. And John Regent began to cry.

"I will let you go now. Please consider my request. I do want to die, and I know you can help."

When John returned to the ranger station, he guessed his tardiness as an hour or more. But he had ten minutes remaining. Rhoda looked up from the desk.

"Back already? Well, I'm starving. Thanks for the extra time." He nodded.

"You look awful. You okay?" Rhoda asked.

"I don't know. Guess I'm getting sick."

"Well, take care of yourself. Here, you can have my Gatorade. Sit."

That night, John fell asleep easily enough, but his slumber turned to a nonstop film reel of violence, hopelessness, and injustice, nightmares that prevented him from rest. These were visions sent by Elvis. For three nights they came like flood waters into John Regent's dreams and scoured his mind again and again. Three days later, Rhoda said, "You look even worse. Why don't you take the day off? I can handle things today. Going to be slow—predicted to be rainy."

"Would you kill someone or something if they asked you to?" John Regent said to Rhoda.

"Huh?"

"Elvis wants to die." John collapsed, losing his grip on wakefulness. Rhoda moved quickly to make sure John was breathing. When she saw that he had lost consciousness, she locked the door and moved John into the back office. She made a pillow of her jacket and laid his head upon it. She wet a towel and placed it on John's brow, which felt hot against her hand. Rain fell heavily now and she watched John's face for discomfort, but he seemed to be breathing normally in a peaceful sleep. Before long, Rhoda lay down beside John and fell asleep too.

It's no surprise that Elvis, though he was unsophisticated

about the ways of men and women, was also cunning. If he were to get his wish, he would have to convince another of his right to die. So he gave Rhoda the same visions. She saw the cavalry, the ferocity of the horses, and the sound of the booming shots. Then she saw the woman with the baby lashed to her breast. Rhoda sobbed as the baby fell, innocent and helpless, into the lake. Rhoda clutched John Regent's hands while in her fitful sleep, if it could be called that. The soldiers charged, Indians retaliated, bears fled, a baby swallowed its weight in water, and his mother clutched at mud as flies landed on her dead body near the edge of the lake. The infant sank to the bottom of the lake and then the lake dried up, the river that fed it for centuries having turned in a new direction. All that remained was a thick, white, chalky layer of ruin and judgments rendered.

Elvis whispered her name just before she woke.

"I want to die. Please help me. I've seen too much and I'm ready to go."

"You're soaked. You've been crying?" John said when he came to.

"I don't know what happened. I saw things I thought I already knew everything about, but it was like I was living inside the memories of others." She trembled.

"Elvis?" John asked.

"Yes."

John put his coat around Rhoda's shoulders. A few minutes later, they rose and reopened the visitor center. A middle-aged man and woman in an RV pulled into the parking lot. They hastily read the interpretive signs and browsed the bookshelves. Then they watched the movie. Thirty minutes later, they were gone.

That night, Rhoda lay in bed, feverish, experiencing the moving images that Elvis sent her. For three nights she suffered the visions. On the fourth night, she woke herself and called John. She had reached her breaking point. John had now counted seven nights of not sleeping.

After work the next day, John and Rhoda began the ascent. John carried the chain saw and Rhoda had safety goggles, gloves, extra gas. Both were on edge and had not been as helpful or professional in demeanor toward visitors as their duties dictated.

"Looks like rain again," said Rhoda.

"That goddamned tree will get cut even if I have to reckon with a towering thundercloud."

But the storm beat them to their destination. Just as they clambered onto the slope, lightning struck Elvis in the center of his trunk, sparking a blue fire. A forceful current of air knocked Rhoda to her knees. John dropped beside her, placing his hand on her back.

"I've never been this tired. I wonder if this is a delusion. I hardly know what's real," he said. Both shook in awe and relief, fright and reverence.

"Good-bye, I'm satisfied—I now see that good of which you spoke," Elvis said.

"You've shown me nothing but pain," Rhoda said, lowering her head.

"You've made your point. We have done so much harm," John said.

"Yes, but I also see your hope. I see your future. Your children, Rhoda and John, the boy and girl that you will have together. I see their lives. You will be proud. They will return water and birds to the lake. The river will run its course once more. I hear the eagle talking about the days to come."

"What are you, some kind of seer?" Rhoda asked.

"Sometimes." Elvis sighed, his stream of breath warming Rhoda and John's faces. "The good grows in some and not in others. But good is there. Been there all along, I guess." Suddenly, the blaze reached an impossible height, flames shooting upward in a terrifying conflagration. Rhoda grabbed for John's hand.

"Let's get out of here!" John shouted above the roar of turbulent, cracking flames. As they climbed into the work truck, Rhoda could see smoke gathering into a mushroom cloud in the rearview mirror.

"It looks like an atomic bomb went off!" she said.

"We need to clear the roads and get down to Big Pine," John said. Rhoda turned the radio knob to the emergency channel. John pulled out onto the road. Just then, lightning flashed across the crest of the Sierra, illuminating the Inyo-White Mountains in exquisite detail. Each bristlecone pine reached for the heavens and inhaled the electric air. Then the rain came down like walls, forcing John Regent to pull over. It was impossible to see in front of the truck. John turned the heat in the truck's cabin to full and pressed the emergency brake into the floorboard. He slid across the seat to Rhoda's side and held her close.

After several minutes, the squall line passed. John put the truck into first gear to continue down to the valley. Once on the highway, John pulled out his cell phone to call the district ranger and report the fire. But before he could dial, he noticed in the distance that Highway 395 seemed to buckle as if animated from beneath. Then a curl formed, like the lip of a wave in the ocean and the road rolled and advanced toward them. John shook his head to reset his eyesight and yelled, "Get down!"

The wave passed under the truck, down Main Street, and out of town. Then it assumed a direct course due south more than two hundred miles to Los Angeles. Richter scale needles ricocheted. Like small fishing vessels in a storm, motorists on Highway 395 drove into the swells, marveling at the tickle in their stomachs as their cars crested each wave. Drivers in their vehicles were lifted, then deposited.

John and Rhoda raised their heads. The road appeared normal.

"Good grows in some," a low-pitched voice said.

"What was that?" John asked.

"Elvis," Rhoda said.

"But not in others," the voice continued. John reversed the truck. When they arrived back at the visitor center they hiked from the parking lot to where Elvis had stood.

"Only Elvis is gone," Rhoda said. "Look, this limb didn't

burn. It's warm." The valley was still, as though holding its breath. The tinny scent of rain mixed with charcoal saturated the air.

At last John spoke. "I wanted him to change his mind."

"I thought he did change his mind, with that rain and that—"

"What was that? The asphalt looked like water."

"Nothing makes sense right now," Rhoda said.

"I'm so tired I could sleep standing up," John said.

"Me too," Rhoda said. They returned to the truck. Rhoda leaned into John and closed her eyes. His head fit neatly on top of hers. Soon, both were asleep. The radio flicked on.

Love me tender, love me long,
take me to your heart.
For it's there that I belong,
and we'll never part.

Acknowledgments

Thank you to my mother Wanda and my father Philip who gave me the gift of nature and the Owens Valley. I'll be forever grateful for the Sierra that you sought and found. To my sister Carol, you let me make up endless exploring games in the backyards of Mammoth Lakes, Bishop, and beyond. Together we could express ourselves and let our imaginations run loose in the complete security beneath Mount Tom. Many friends and family offered hospitality and comfortable places in which to research and write— Nancy and Dick Wood, Rinnie Nardone, Rebecca Bryson and Jack Landy, Miriam Seger, Ted Bosley, Carol and Todd Underhill, and Marisela and Kelly Martinez. I spent a glorious week working on these stories in the Cascades thanks to Oregon State University's long-term ecological reflections program residency.

For your support, expertise, inspiration, and advice, thank you to Amy Sabbadini, Beth Seetch, Phil Pister,

D.C. Jackson, Dave Livermore, Rachel Brown Gazaui, Stephen Lammers, Bill Landreth, Michael Prather, Geoff McQuilken, Karen and Michael McArdle, Andy Gottlieb, Kay and Marshall Wolff, Dave Carle, Pat Lathrop, Micaela Heekin, Lindsie Bear, Genny Smith, Tracy Wood, Laura Crane, Jessica Hoffman and Jose Benavides, Annie Ho and Patrick Ting, Stella Egar, Mike Sweeney, Elizabeth Snider, Mari Marjamaa, Tim Fox, Wendy Mills, Christine Lee, Paula Litchfield, Mark Stephan, Greg Rynne, Nicole Rice, Kate Frazer Devokaitis, Sylvia Busby Stone, John Zablocki, Maria D'Amato, Garrett Mettler, Adam and Edith Barker, Maricar Boyle, Jessica Leas, Jennifer Riddle Harding, Jordan Peavey, Wendy Pulling, Jan Nicholas, Mark Reynolds, Holly Fink, Karen Eller and Greg Sherman, Kirk Klausmeyer, Alex Mas, Scott Morrison, Debbie Begley, Audrey Langan, Tripti Thomas, Wendy Corr, Tauni Sauvage, and my second Mom, Joan McCrossen. To my storytelling aunts Shirley and Connie, you showed me how a tale well told could make someone crack up, or crack them wide open. To the children I love being an aunt to more than anything, may you take the reins of protecting our planet with joy and purpose: Emily, Michael, Todd, Caroline, and Sammy.

For excellent staffs who helped me with source documents, books, history, science, and experience—The Eastern California Museum, Lafayette College, Spellbinder Books, Manzanar National Historic Site, Eastern Sierra Interpretive Association, Bureau of Land Management, Inyo National Forest, University of California, Yosemite National Park,

Museum of Western Film History, Ancient Bristlecone Pine Forest, Bodie State Historic Park, The Nature Conservancy, Los Angeles Department of Water and Power, Yosemite Conservancy, and the Mono Lake Committee.

These stories first had an audience in the classrooms of Otis Haschemeyer at the Writing Salon in San Francisco, now of the University of Oregon, and Debbie Danielpour of Harvard University Extension, now of Boston University, both of whom gave early encouragement and productive feedback. Through answering an ad in *Poets & Writers* I found a tremendous editor and partner in Laurie Scheer of the University of Wisconsin. My copy editor Natalie Karst is a trusted advisor, not only in the use of the Oxford comma but in ensuring consistency. I am deeply appreciative of all the people who helped catch errors or omissions.

The writing and reading community, especially the editorial boards of independent literary journals, assisted me in so many ways with compassionate editing, encouragement, and the chance to be read. I am deeply grateful for these people, who are often unpaid but are passionate about writing and promoting authors, especially Caleb True of Dynamo Verlag Press.

Finally, I am thankful for our nation's deepest valley. The Owens Valley is heaven to me and to so many who drive Highway 395 with the majesty of two mountain chains outside the windows, cradling us like the children of nature and creation that we are.

To learn more, please visit—

Author website
www.kristinezeigler.com

Author blog
www.owensrivergirl.com